Small Kid, Big Legend

YOUNG
FiOnN

For baby Patrick, x

Small Kid, Big Legend

YOUNG FiOnN

RONAN MOORE

ILLUSTRATED BY ALEXANDRA COLOMBO

Gill Books

Gill Books
Hume Avenue
Park West
Dublin 12
www.gillbooks.ie

Gill Books is an imprint of M.H. Gill and Co.

Text © Ronan Moore 2020
Illustrations © Alexandra Colombo 2020

978 07171 85863

Designed by iota (www.iota-books.ie).
Proofread by Emma Dunne.

Printed by CPI Group (UK) Ltd,
Croydon CR0 4YY
This book is typeset in IM Fell.

The paper used in this book comes from
the wood pulp of managed forests. For
every tree felled, at least one tree is planted,
thereby renewing natural resources.

A CIP catalogue record for this book is
available from the British Library.

5 4 3 2 1

CONTENTS

HOW TO PRONOUNCE THE NAMES IN THIS BOOK

Abcán	Ow-cawn
Áed (Goll) Mac Morna	Ay (Gull) Mock Mor-na
Aillen Mac Miona	Ayl-lane Mock Mee-na
Amhairghin	Av-argeen
Anlon	An-lun
Aoife	Ee-feh
Beirgín	Ber-geen
Bodhmall	Bow-mul
Breac	Brack
Cana	Khan-a

Cearbhall	Car-ool
Clan Bascna	Clawn Bweesh-cna
Clan Morna	Clawn More-na
Cnes	Kin-ass
Conn	Con
Crimmal	Crim-mal
Cumhall	Coo-al
Dealra Dubh	Jal-rav Duh
Demne	Jev-neh
Dúban	Dhoo-bawn
Dúnán	Dhoo-nawn
Emain Macha	Ow-win Mah-kha
Fiacha	Fee-ack-ha
Fianna	Fee-ana
Finnegas	Finn-ay-gus

Fionn Mac Cumhaill	F-yun Mock Coo-al
Fomorians	Fo-more-ee-ans
Gadra	Guy-ra
Garb	Garv or Garu
Gobán	Go-bawn
Ilbrach	Ill-brock
Iollan	Ull-an
Lochan	Lough-an
Lonán	Lunn-awn
Luachra	Luah-khir
Luchet	Loo-khayd
Mac Cecht	Mock Kay-ukht
Mac Cuill	Mock Quill
Mac Gréine	Mock Grey-nge
Manannán	Monn-a-nawn

Milesians	My-lee-shuns
Muintir Cessair	Mween-thir Khay-ser
Muirne	Mwir-na
Neacht	Ny-akht
Nóe	No-eh
Odar	Ow-ar
Phelim	Fail-im
Rian	Ree-an
Rígán	Ree-gawn
Samhain	Sow-win
Tadg	Thy-ig
Tuatha Dé Danann	Thu-ha Jay Dhan-unn
Uallgarg	Ooll-ghor-eg

PROLOGUE

In ancient times, Ireland was ruled by the Celts, a race of people who lived in a land of myths and legends, warriors and druids, monsters and magic. Many extraordinary and epic events took place during the period in which the Celts lived, but over the hundreds and hundreds of years that followed, many of these tales were lost to the mists of time.

However, some stories have survived.

The most famous of these are the tales of Fionn Mac Cumhaill and the Fianna, a mighty band of warriors that fought on behalf of the High King, who was responsible for protecting the people of Ireland. How Fionn succeeded in becoming the leader of the most famous band of Fianna to have ever lived is a tale of love and loss, war and revenge, family and friendship — and a young boy with a warrior's heart.

But before we embark on this adventure with Fionn, we must go back to the very beginning — to the story of a girl named Muirne.

THE DRUID'S DAUGHTER

'**M**uirne! Muirne, my dear? My lovely daughter? My little darling? MUIRNE! MUIRNE! MUIRNEEEEEE!'

The calls of the Chief Druid resounded through the palace. He had been looking for Muirne all morning. She was probably getting up to no good in the Forbidden Forest, Tadg thought to himself. He was determined to put an end to her free-spirited ways. That night, in his palace of Almu, on the plains of Kildare, he would hold the great feast of Samhain to celebrate the end of the harvest season. And to this feast he had invited the wealthiest men in all of Ireland. One of these men would marry his daughter — and he would be finally rid of her.

1

As the sound of his footsteps disappeared down the corridor away from her room, his fair-haired daughter Muirne crept out from beneath a pile of cloaks in the corner. She didn't like her father. In fact, she hated him. He was mean and cruel and treated her terribly. Tadg only called Muirne his 'lovely daughter' when he wanted something. And today he wanted her to marry, which she had only found out about that morning.

Knowing that Tadg might soon return, Muirne wasted no time in climbing out her bedroom window and running into the neighbouring woods. There was someone deep in the forest whom she urgently needed to talk to.

• • •

Muirne didn't know why her father disliked her so much. Some said he blamed her for his wife's death: she had first fallen ill when she was giving birth to Muirne. Others said that, in a failed attempt to save his wife's life, he had fallen under the spell of an evil spirit that had cloaked his heart in darkness. Whatever the reason, he had always treated Muirne dreadfully. He had prohibited her from mixing with any children her own age and rarely allowed her to leave the palace. Most important, he had instructed her that under no circumstances was she to enter the Forbidden Forest, which bordered Almu to the east and ran all the way to the banks of the River Boyne. This was her favourite rule to disobey.

Only the mighty Fianna were allowed enter the forest. Not even Tadg dared tell the High King — a man by the name of Conn of the Hundred Battles — where his personal fighting force, made up of the most fearless warriors in the land, could or could not hunt. The Fianna warriors often spoke of their fear of the evil spirits that inhabited the trees. But it wasn't evil spirits that Muirne had encountered late one evening many years before, but the kindly Bodhmall and Breac.

These two old women had brought Muirne back to their small hut of mud and willow branches that was hidden away in the heart of the woods. They had fed her a hearty meal, given her a bed and led her back out of the forest the next day. It was the first ounce of kindness that Muirne had ever experienced. And just like a sapling looking for light, from that day on, at any chance Muirne got, she would escape into the woods to be nourished by their warmth and care.

Time passed and Bodhmall and Breac grew to treat her like a daughter. For almost a decade, she visited them regularly and they showed her all the ways of the wild — how to hunt, how to hide, how to swim and how to survive. They even showed her how to talk to the animals —

the good ones, at least. And for ten years, from four to fourteen, she was happy in their care.

This joyful time did not last forever. In the winter of her fourteenth year, Muirne was spotted leaving the forest by Áed Mac Morna, head of Clan Morna and member of the Fianna. While the Fianna were known to be just, fair and gallant, there were exceptions. And Áed and his men were a family of exceptions. Áed was not only the Fianna's strongest warrior, but also its most fierce, vile and wicked. Every winter, he and his men would spend the cold months under Tadg's roof. His arch-rivals — Clan Bascna — would be among the Fianna forces who would shelter with the High King in Tara.

Áed had heard Tadg complain bitterly that his daughter was sneaking into the forest against his will, so Áed decided that he would find out what she was doing there. His search brought him to the camp of Bodhmall and Breac. When he reported this to Tadg, the Chief Druid was outraged and sent Áed and his band of merciless men galloping into the woods with just one order — kill the old women and return with their heads.

A few days later, Muirne managed to escape Almu to visit her friends. But she found nothing of Bodhmall and Breac in their camp. Just broken pots and pans, torn sheets and scattered clothes. Áed, she later learned, had not succeeded in killing the pair. However, it would be the last that anyone would hear of Bodhmall and Breac for a long, long time.

As Muirne sat remembering her friends, she found herself looking at the flowing current of the River Boyne. It was said that a magical fish swam in the river's depths and that whoever caught and tasted it would be rewarded with all the knowledge in the world. Indeed, this fish was the reason Tadg had conquered this land. However, after twenty years of trying, Tadg had caught nothing more than a bad cold from the river and had long since given up trying to catch the fabled Salmon of Knowledge. Only Muirne had ever successfully fished something out of the river, but it wasn't a fish that she had caught. Instead, it was a boy named Cumhall. And it was this unlikely catch that she was stealing into the forest to speak to.

It had been just over four years since they met. Cumhall had been hunting with a small band of young Fianna warriors when a wild boar they were chasing entered the forest. Captivated by the pursuit and already tasting the boar rashers he would have for the next day's breakfast, he followed it until it brought him to the banks of the Boyne. Suddenly something spooked Cumhall's horse. It reared up and sent him head over heels towards the water. Landing on the rocky bank, Cumhall was knocked out. Before his friends could reach him, he was swept into the rapidly flowing river. The Boyne, heavy and angry after days of summer downpours, quickly carried him away.

Cumhall was the most promising of the young Fianna warriors. He was brave without fear, skilled without limit, a powerful swimmer and probably the most handsome of the Fianna (which wasn't hard — they were a rough and ready lot). But none of that is any use when you are unconscious. He would surely have drowned had it not been for Muirne. Spying him from the riverbank, she swiftly dived in and, using the oxter bag under his arm, dragged him onto the riverbank. A half-drowned Cumhall soon awoke, spluttering up water. It took some minutes before he managed to regain his composure. After all, aside from nearly drowning, a member of the Fianna should not need to be rescued — they were fearless warriors! Embarrassed, he turned to thank the boy who had secured his life — only to be shocked that it wasn't a boy at all.

'A girl!' he exclaimed.

'Yes, a girl,' Muirne repeated. 'I'm glad your eyesight hasn't been affected. You know, when someone saves your life, it's polite to say thank you.'

'Uhh ... oh ... I'm sorry, thank you. I was just surprised you're a girl, that's all.'

'Why?'

'Well … there are no girls in the Fianna, and I never saw a girl do anything like that.'

'Well,' Muirne snapped back, 'I'll have you know that just because girls can't join your silly all-boys club, that doesn't mean a thing. I can do anything a boy can do and more!'

Although he was grateful that his life had just been saved, Cumhall wasn't used to having his beloved Fianna bad-mouthed. And certainly not from a jumped-up know-it-all like her, with her wit, poise and intelligence … and striking fair hair … and arresting face. Cumhall collected himself and retorted, 'Girls are better than boys? You must be kidding me?'

'We are!'

'Prove it then,' Cumhall declared.

'Fine,' said Muirne. 'Let's hold five tests of our skills. The first of us to win three tests will prove once and for all who is the best.'

Cumhall agreed. 'Sure. Let's start tomorrow then. Midday for our first test?'

'Second test,' Muirne corrected him. 'Swimming today was our first test, and I think we can agree who won that. One-nil to the girls, I'd say. Go home, get dry and I'll meet you here tomorrow for round two. And,' she added with a grin, 'don't tell anyone.'

'Don't worry,' he pouted. 'I won't.' Just then, he could hear the voices of his older brother Crimmal and his kinsmen Dúnán and Luchet calling his name. All of them were of Clan Bascna — an extended family that supplied the Fianna with many warriors.

'Hey! I'm over here,' Cumhall shouted in their direction. When he turned back to Muirne, she was already gone.

• • •

The next day, Cumhall returned to the forest. This time, before Muirne could open her mouth, he announced the second challenge — strength. He led Muirne up the riverbank until they reached a large clearing where more than a dozen great big granite boulders lay.

'Right, these are called the Ogre's Boulders. Every full moon the Fianna come down here to work out by lifting and throwing these great rocks. Today's test is a race to see who can carry one of these boulders up and around that old holly bush there in the distance. The only rule is that once you lift one you can't let it down again until you're back in the clearing.'

Although Muirne might have been small for her age, she was tough, so the sight of the boulders didn't worry her. 'What are you waiting for?' she asked Cumhall.

'Right,' Cumhall replied. 'On your mark ... get set ... GO!'

And with that they took off – but not in the same direction! Muirne immediately bent down, wrapped her arms around a giant stone, rose up and started moving quickly towards the tree. Meanwhile, instead of lifting his own boulder, Cumhall stuck his hands into the thick, dark, gluey mud on the riverbank. He watched Muirne building up a steady lead. By the time he lifted a boulder Muirne was almost at the tree, but Cumhall knew her lead wouldn't last.

As she rounded the old holly bush, she knew she was in trouble. Although she had a good head start on Cumhall, her grip on the large boulder was slipping as her hands were beginning to sweat. With every step she struggled more and more to hold on to the heavy rock. The closer she got to the clearing, the slicker the boulder became. All the while, Cumhall was closing the gap. With his hands caked in dried mud, he was holding his boulder tightly and marching slowly and steadily towards her. He came closer, closer, closer, until he passed her out only five steps from the entrance to the clearing. He threw down his stone with a great cheer of 'Go on, ya boyo!'

This time it was Muirne's turn to feel hard done by. She barely shook his hand before storming off, shouting back as she went, 'Same time tomorrow for round three. Bring your best bow and arrow.'

• • •

The following day came Muirne's chance for revenge. 'Right,' she announced, 'over there, at the edge of the river some fifty steps away, I've marked a cross on that great aspen. Three shots. Whoever lands closest to the target wins. I'll let you go first.'

Although Cumhall was good, his first shot failed to hit the mark. Muirne then stepped forward and took aim. But just as she was about to fire, she closed her eyes and allowed the soft breeze to brush her face. Then, with a hint of a smile, she changed her aim ever so slightly. And let fly.

THUNG.

The sound of the arrow hitting the target echoed through the clearing. Muirne opened her eyes to see a direct hit. Each time Cumhall shot an arrow, he came closer. But he couldn't match Muirne. Going into the penultimate challenge she now led two to one.

• • •

On the fourth day, they tested their speed with a dash from a wizened old rowan tree back to their clearing.

'One, two ... GO!' Muirne shouted as she took off, shouldering Cumhall into the forest floor as she went.

However, despite thinking that she was meant to say 'three' before shouting 'go', as well as contending with a mouthful of leaves, Cumhall soon caught up with her. Fleet-footed as she was, Cumhall was just that bit quicker. Bounding over fallen logs with ease, he made it across the finishing line ahead of Muirne by just the width of a feather.

'Two-all then.' Cumhall beamed as he caught his breath.

'Yes, two-all.'

'So, what will be the final test?'

Muirne thought for a moment before responding. 'Intelligence.'

Cumhall quickly disagreed. 'No, endurance.'

They argued back and forth until finally, with a smirk, Muirne relented. 'Right, endurance it is, but I get to decide the endurance task.'

'That sounds fair,' Cumhall answered. 'But what does the winner get?'

Muirne, now smiling even wider, replied, 'The loser will have to carry out one task for the winner every day for a moon cycle.'

'You're on,' Cumhall retorted. 'I better start drawing up my list of what I want you to do.'

That evening, as she pondered the final test, Muirne realised her cheeks were a little sore but couldn't work out why. Finally, it came to her. It was because she had been smiling so much of late — something she couldn't remember doing in a long, long time.

• • •

The next day, they met for the fifth — and final — task.

'For endurance,' Muirne began, 'we will be doing press-ups. However, rather than us both doing press-ups at the same time, we will declare how many we think we can do without stopping to rest. Whoever declares the most and is then able to do them all wins.'

Cumhall's eyes lit up. He loved press-ups and could do them all day long. Indeed, he was the best of all the Fianna at them and was certain that victory was his. Without even allowing Muirne the chance to say her number, he announced, 'Six hundred and one! I will do six hundred and one press-ups.'

'Okay then,' she replied. But just as Cumhall started to get down on his knees, Muirne said, 'I will do between eight and nine hundred.'

Cumhall's jaw dropped.

'I can do between eight and nine hundred,' she repeated. 'Do you want to see me try or would you like to declare a higher number?'

Cumhall knew he could not beat that – not in one go. 'N-n-no, go ahead then. Let's see you do it.'

Muirne tied her hair up with a sprig of wildflower, knelt down and began. 'One – two – three – four – five – six – seven – eight – nine. Okay, I think I'll stop there.' She stood up.

'What!' exclaimed Cumhall. 'You said you can do between eight and nine hundred. You've only done nine!'

'I know,' Muirne responded merrily. 'And if you ask any of your friends, they'll tell you that nine is a number between eight and nine hundred.' And with that, Muirne gave him a list for the first week's tasks. 'Number one – gathering honeysuckle. I like the smell of honeysuckle and a nice bunch would do wonders for my room.'

Cumhall never did ask his friends about the number nine, nor did he tell them about the honeysuckle. He returned every afternoon without fail to complete whatever task Muirne had set for him: make her a bowl from an uprooted sycamore tree, bring her a basket of wild strawberries, repair a tear in her favourite cloak. No matter what she asked of him, Cumhall completed it and never complained.

On the last day of the moon cycle, they met for what was to be Cumhall's final task.

'I have one final request,' Muirne started.

'You know your twenty-eight days are up,' Cumhall replied.

'I know. That's why I waited,' she continued. 'This time you're allowed to say no.'

'What is it?'

'Would you like to continue collecting honeysuckle for me?' she smiled.

Cumhall's face broke into a wide grin. 'Yes. Yes, I would.'

● ● ●

And that is how the parents of Fionn, the most famous Fianna warrior ever, fell in love. And in the four years that followed Muirne grew into the strong and confident young woman who Bodhmall and Breac had hoped she would become. Meanwhile, Cumhall became the youngest ever leader of the Fianna by defeating Áed in a wrestling match, continuing the long line of proud Fianna leaders that came from Clan Bascna. Throughout all this time, except to Crimmal and some of their closest friends, their love had remained a well-guarded secret.

Until now. Tadg's plans to marry Muirne off to one of Ireland's most unappealing men would change everything. Slipping unnoticed past the workers preparing that night's feast, she was struck by an idea. Maybe it could work, but first she had to find Cumhall.

• • •

'What is it?' Cumhall asked, taking Muirne's hand in his own.

'Tonight, at the feast of Samhain, I am to be married. My father has arranged for three men to come and sit with me during the banquet. At the end of the feast, one of them will claim me as his wife.'

'Why?' wondered Cumhall. 'Why now?'

'My father wants rid of me. These men have gold; my father has influence with the High King. It is a good trade as far as they are concerned.'

'That's a pity,' Cumhall said sheepishly. 'I was kind of hoping you'd marry me.'

'I was hoping that as well,' Muirne replied, a little red of cheek.

'Well then, we're just going to have to escape.'

'And what of the Fianna?' Muirne asked.

Cumhall looked across the Boyne, flowing rapidly

below, before turning his gaze back to Muirne. 'They'll get over me,' he declared. 'But how will we escape?'

'Don't worry,' Muirne responded. 'I've had an idea. Just make sure you are at the entrance to the forest with your fastest horse by the feast's end – I will take care of the rest.'

● ● ●

That afternoon, Muirne was back in Almu helping to prepare food for the feast. As she chopped and stirred, she sang quietly to herself. It was only a few hours before the first guests would arrive and there was still much to do. Servants ran back and forth with great gusto and energy carrying wooden bowls filled to the brim with nettle and mutton broth. But the cheerful whistling, humming and singing abruptly stopped when Tadg appeared in the kitchen's entrance, ready to cast an eye over proceedings.

Muirne approached her father. 'I'm sorry I missed you earlier, dear father. I heard the wonderful news of my upcoming marriage. I'm terribly excited. I've been helping out here for a while and I might go and get ready for tonight, if you don't mind?'

'Of course, er ... my dear,' Tadg answered, surprised at her new-found politeness. 'Off you go and remember that the first course will be at sunset, so don't be late.' He was pleasantly surprised. It seemed that his daughter had finally learnt some manners. As Tadg reflected on this sudden change, he noticed a servant standing uneasily beside him holding half a length of rope.

'What is it?' rumbled Tadg.

'The goat, Chief Druid. The goat for tonight's feast. It's ... disappeared.'

Looking at the rope that had held the goat, Tadg scowled. He had been looking forward to having some goat for dinner. 'Right, we'll just to have to make do with boar.'

● ● ●

Muirne took her seat at the top table. She was wearing her most elegant pair of shoes: clogs that had been exquisitely crafted from a fallen ash tree. She had also replaced her well-worn tunic with a dress that had once belonged to her mother. It was made of the finest wool patterned with the dye of wild juniper berries. She had let loose her long fair hair and had tucked a sprig of honeysuckle behind her ear. She looked beautiful in the clear, crisp late-October night.

Beside her sat the first of the suitors: Odar. Unlike Muirne, he was not beautiful. In fact, Old Odar must have been at least three times her age and then some.

He had grey hairs sprouting not only from his head, but from his ears and nose too! He owned a huge ironworks on the banks of the River Shannon, where he had made all his money from making swords and spears. Despite having three wives (and thirteen children!) he felt it was now time to marry for the fourth time.

Although Muirne had never met him before, she had heard there was one thing he could not tolerate: garlic. Muirne had made sure that before she had left the kitchen she had put plenty of wild garlic into their starter. Old Odar left his soup untouched while Muirne merrily slurped, burped and belched her way through hers, talking right into old Odar's face! The scent of garlic left him green. By the second course poor old Odar was glad to be gone.

Next up was Nóe, the son of a wealthy chief from the foothills of the Sperrin Mountains of Tyrone, who made his money buying and selling gold and silver. Nóe was known as the 'golden child'. This was not only because of his work but also because he was one of the most handsome men in all of Ireland. However, the problem with him was that the person who loved Nóe the most was ... Nóe. And talking about himself was Nóe's favourite conversation.

As they commenced their mains of wild boar and elderflower jus, Nóe started a long-winded story about how wonderful he was. But just as he began talking, Muirne did a very unusual thing. She started to hum. Not a loud, sing-song hum, like when you are doing something that you enjoy. No, instead it was the soft, you-can't-quite-tell-where-it-is-coming-from type of hum that drives druids, teachers and suitors crazy!

Nóe immediately stopped talking, convinced that he could hear something. But just as he stopped, Muirne stopped too. And every time Nóe would begin to talk, again Muirne would start humming. It became so unsettling for Nóe that he started to think he was going a little mad. Very soon Nóe grew silent, and they finished their dinner in perfect peace and quiet.

While this was all happening, Tadg, who had been looking on from his table, was starting to get angry. He could see from the reaction of the first two suitors that Muirne was back to her normal impudent self — and that his idea was not going to plan. Still, there was one more suitor to sit with her for dessert: Dúban.

Dúban, or Dúban the Dreary as he was known to his friends (of which there were few), was the son of a wealthy chief in the west in Sligo who lived in the shadow of the Ox Mountains. He was said to have as many cattle as hairs on his head. Dúban was neither as self-centred as Nóe nor as old as Odar, but he was dreadfully boring. He never joked or laughed and all he wanted to talk about were the rise and fall in cattle prices, herbal remedies to cure cows of illnesses, and the difference between the grass in the midlands and that of the hilly variety. Muirne had the perfect plan for this: the more boring the conversation, the sleepier she would act. Every time he mentioned cows, cattle, udders or heifers, Muirne would yawn, rub her eyes and at one stage she pretended to nod off. It didn't take long for Dúban to become very annoyed that she seemed entirely uninterested in the fascinating subject of Ireland's most majestic and noble creatures.

By the time the meal was over, all three suitors were suitably unimpressed. More unimpressed, however, was Tadg. And he couldn't hide his fury any longer.

'MUIRNE!' he roared, bringing the celebration to a shuddering halt. 'Get yourself up to your room, you ... you ...' With all eyes from the feast now on him, he forced the tightest of smiles before finishing '... wonderful girl'. And with that, off she skipped.

Tadg then turned to his three hundred guests. 'Er ... apologies everyone. Nothing to be concerned about. I just remembered something very important that Muirne forgot to do, soooo ... continue enjoying yourselves and I will be right back.' He beckoned to Áed. 'Lock her in her room, Áed. Don't let her leave. I'll be up soon — with whomever of these unfortunate men I can still persuade to marry her.' Áed grunted in agreement. However, by the time he got to her room, Muirne had already closed the door behind her. Putting his ear to the keyhole, Áed could hear her clopping about in her wooden clogs. Safe in the knowledge that she was inside, he locked the door, folded his arms and stood guard in the hall. When Tadg arrived half an hour later, she was still clopping about. With him was Odar, the only suitor who had agreed to take her (at a much-reduced price).

'Once again, Odar, do let me apologise for the soup. I have no idea how it could have happened, but when I find out who is responsible, I will send their head south and their body north. Oh, here we are! This is Áed. He helps keep everyone safe.' Tadg quietly whispered to the half-giant, 'Has she tried to leave?'

'No, Chief Druid,' Áed muttered. 'She has been clopping about this whole time.'

'Good,' replied Tadg. 'Well, let me tell her the good news.'

Áed unlocked her room and the Chief Druid entered. But no sooner had he gone in when a great cry shook the beams of the palace. Áed and Odar ran into the room. They looked first at Tadg, who was crimson with fury, and then at Tadg's missing goat, who had two wooden clogs tied to its front hooves.

• • •

Far away from Almu, Cumhall urged his galloping horse on as Muirne held her love tight. As they escaped into the night, she could swear she heard her name being shouted in the wind. 'Muirne! Muirne! MUIRNEEEEEE!'

THE BATTLE OF CNUCHA

'Father, don't leave me!'

'I won't, son!'

But the fair-haired boy began to drift into the darkness as the sound of galloping hooves grew louder.

'Father!' the child cried once more.

'Don't go! Hold on!' Cumhall roared. Over the clatter of hooves, he could hear human voices.

'Father!'

'Demne!'

Cumhall woke with a start, covered in sweat. He had been dreaming again. For two seasons now he had been having the same dream, each time growing more distinct. When the dreams had begun, the boy had been only a baby, crying as it faded into the darkness. With each successive vision the boy grew older and the scene became more vivid. One thing, however, remained the same – Cumhall was uncertain what it all meant.

He turned to his wife, Muirne. But she was gone. Judging by the cold patch on their makeshift bed of moss where she had lain, she had been gone for a while. He huddled closer to their small campfire, its russet embers still providing a thin blanket of warmth. The mist of the nearby river had encroached during the night. The haze made it difficult to see anyone coming towards them, but Cumhall wasn't worried. This area, Fassadinin, in the north of Kilkenny, was known for being uninhabited. In the week they had been here they saw and heard no one. It was a welcome respite.

To his right, his old friend Dúnán was snoring away. Beside Dúnán, the bright, fair hair of Luchet was poking out from beneath his sheepskin cover. On the other side of the fire, Cumhall's older brother Crimmal lay slumbering. The three men had joined Muirne and Cumhall soon after the couple's escape from Almu and had been their constant companions and guardians ever since.

• • •

Two years previously, Muirne had left her father, Chief Druid Tadg, to run off and marry Cumhall. Outraged at his daughter's defiance, and embarrassed and insulted in front of his esteemed visitors and Muirne's would-be husband, he had immediately demanded Cumhall's head. 'He has broken our laws. Your laws, my king. The laws that govern us. He must be executed,' he had publicly proclaimed to Conn of the Hundred Battles, High King of Ireland.

Conn knew that what Cumhall had done was wrong: he had broken one of the Fianna's most sacred rules — that they would never take anyone's hand in marriage — but Cumhall had been a brave and loyal warrior. Conn owed victory in many of his hundred battles to Cumhall's efforts, and under his leadership the Fianna had enjoyed a golden age of success. He didn't want to have Cumhall killed, but Conn recognised that disobedience had to be punished.

'You are right, Chief Druid,' Conn admitted, 'Cumhall has broken the law of this land. He will be dealt with. However, under that same law, I give him until the full moon to repent. If he brings Muirne home safely and asks for forgiveness, I will spare his life. Muirne can live out her days with you, in captivity if you so wish. Cumhall will be banished from these shores — never to return.'

After pronouncing his judgement, Conn had turned to Crimmal, who had been sitting in the shadows listening intently. 'Crimmal, son of Trenmor, brother of Cumhall, you know your blood better than anyone else. You have heard what I have uttered this evening. Take three men and set out to find Cumhall and Muirne. Explain to them their options. Counsel them to make the right choice — or face the consequences.' Conn swept angrily out of the chamber, knowing that the leader of the Fianna warriors was soon to be either executed or exiled.

After Conn's departure, Tadg stood at the entrance to his palace, staring into the darkness of the night sky. A blackness also shrouded his soul. He had no interest in welcoming back his daughter. While he had long ago lost any love in his heart for her, he now wanted every trace of her, and the shame she had brought on him, wiped from the earth. He turned on his heel and strode towards the innermost chambers of his palace, where he kept his most sacred and secret texts.

• • •

As Tadg ran his finger over the ancient texts his mind drifted momentarily to when Muirne had been born. It was then that his life had changed forever, though Tadg could no longer remember that, just as he could not recall the kind and loving man he had once been or the wise, young druid that Conn had entrusted to become his Chief Druid. The reason he had no memory of any of these was because of the supernatural Dealra Dubh — the evilest entity known to mortals.

The Dealra Dubh had arrived into Tadg's life at the same time as Muirne. His wife at this time was called Almu. Very soon after she had given birth, she became gravely ill, and not even the druids could save her. They told Tadg that there was no kindly spirit that they could call upon for help and that he should spend these last few moments saying goodbye.

Tadg loved his wife more than life itself and refused to let her go. He decided that if no kindly spirits would save her, he would call on the cruellest one instead — the Dealra Dubh. The Dealra Dubh was an evil spectre of death that hovered between this realm and the next, bringing tragedy to those who were unlucky enough to cross its path. It was said that it appeared as a figure in a cloak as black as the darkest of winter nights, with only its pair of sickly yellow eyes visible.

Deep in one of his sacred texts, Tadg had found a magical incantation to call it forth. And that is what he did, pleading for it to save his beloved. It agreed but extracted the highest of prices: it took Tadg's soul and cloaked with eternal darkness any love he might have for his newly born daughter. As for Almu, she did survive, but the Dealra Dubh gave her only one year. During that time, the sparkle that once burnt in her eyes had dimmed. She became merely a ghost of her past self.

After her death, Tadg built a gilded palace and named it after her. With each passing year, he began to call on this shadowy figure more and more to aid him in his sorcery. And with each spell, the Dealra Dubh's influence over him grew — until he became the evil man who Muirne knew as her father.

Tadg didn't want Cumhall to be forgiven or his daughter to be returned. He wanted them both dead. In Áed Mac Morna, who knew that the Fianna were his now to lead, Tadg had the perfect henchman. But killing Cumhall would not be an easy thing. Along with his agility, strength, skill and speed, Cumhall had an oxter bag filled with treasure that he carried under his arm that helped make him one of the fiercest warriors in the land. It was a magical bag, passed from one generation of Clan Bascna to the next. When Cumhall needed something, he could reach into it and it would magically appear. It had got him out of the tightest of corners. He just had to reach in and pull out what he needed: flint for fire, a shield to protect, a sling and stones to hunt, a healing potion to recover, some food to keep going a day longer, not to mention the many magical weapons that were stored inside.

Tadg knew that he could use the black magic of the Dealra Dubh to enchant a spear hewn from a holly tree. This spear would be the oxter bag's evil equal.

· · ·

Following Conn's orders, Crimmal and the warriors Dúnán, Luchet and Fiacha rode through the night until they caught up with Muirne and Cumhall. In the shade of a woodland glen, they found the couple and alerted them to Conn's demands. Muirne and Cumhall both gave the same response: the only way they would now ever be separated would be by the sword.

Two days later, the solitary figure of Fiacha emerged on the horizon. Although all four of the Fianna had wanted to stay and protect the two lovers, someone had to return to Conn. It was Fiacha, the only one among them not related to Clan Bascna by blood, who had been chosen. Cumhall had explained what he wanted Fiacha to report to Conn, and he also asked Fiacha to keep a close eye on the High King, to whom Cumhall remained loyal. He then handed Fiacha a spear with a leaf-shaped arrowhead that had been passed down through generations of Clan Bascna, requesting he hold on to it until Cumhall's return, before finally wishing him well.

As Conn watched this lone figure's approach, he guessed what Cumhall's reply had been. He assembled the Fianna and announced, 'Cumhall has chosen neither to return nor to repent, so I must declare him an outlaw.

However, winter has now come so we will not be able to fight. Clan Bascna will be among the Fianna to stay here with me. Clan Morna will stay in Almu until the snows clear. Under the direction of Áed Mac Morna, the new leader of the Fianna, you will bring Cumhall to justice — and Muirne back to the Chief Druid.'

However, Tadg and Áed would not have their revenge the following year. On the first day of spring, the High King awoke to find that many of his Fianna warriors had deserted him. Every member of Clan Bascna, who had stayed the winter in Tara, had left in the dead of night. They resolved that, rather than hunting him down, they would find Cumhall and fight in his service.

But they did not find him. Muirne, Cumhall and their loyal companions had hidden their tracks well. They would travel unobserved across the land for two more years. Following the rivers of Ireland, sleeping under the night sky, always ready to move at a hint of danger.

They had spent that first winter travelling along the banks of the River Brosna. As spring broke the group moved down the great Shannon and then downstream to the River Maigue before spending much of the summer rounding the inlets of Kerry and Cork. The following winter, they gradually moved eastwards along the three sister waterways of the Barrow, the Nore and the Suir.

Throughout that time, Clan Bascna had moved westwards, hoping to find Cumhall in the Kingdom of Connacht. As they searched, they were forced to fight the Fianna forces led by Clan Morna that the High King had ordered to follow them. During these months, the outnumbered forces of Clan Bascna lost many men. The skirmishes would continue through the summer until the High King called back Áed and most of his forces to prepare for a war with a chieftain in Scotland who was threatening Ireland's northern shores.

During that autumn, as Clan Bascna licked their wounds out west, as smaller parties of Áed's men continued to keep watch for signs of Muirne and Cumhall, and as the High King and the rest of the Fianna strengthened their northern defences, Muirne became pregnant.

While she had not known many women who had been pregnant, Muirne knew from an early stage that she was with child. Being sick four mornings in a row was a strong first clue. Not wanting to worry Cumhall, she blamed their breakfast of fish from the River Nore, which Luchet had cooked. The following week she found herself demanding that Cumhall sleep on the other side of the camp, such was the stench of salmon from his breath. As the weeks continued, she began to rest more, was less able to accompany Cumhall hunting and lost her temper over the smallest things.

'What is wrong, my love?' Cumhall finally asked one evening when he was feeling particularly brave.

'Nothing is wrong,' Muirne responded. 'The problem is that everything is right.'

'I don't understand?' Cumhall said, confused.

Muirne took his hand and laid it on her bump. 'I'm pregnant, my dear.' And with that, they both laughed, then hugged, then smiled — and then cried. Finally, both asked in unison, 'What do we do now?'

● ● ●

Cumhall was jolted from this fond memory by a voice behind him.

'Morning, my dear.'

He swivelled around to see Muirne enter their secluded dell carrying a breakfast of hare, mushrooms and thyme. Although she was now eight months pregnant, she was still light-footed enough to catch breakfast.

'Couldn't sleep?' asked Cumhall.

'Yes, I just can't get back to sleep when I wake, even with the help of Dúnán's melodic snoring.'

'I don't snore,' retorted Dúnán, turning back over in his bed.

'Snore? Of course you snore,' Muirne called over to him. 'You sound like a drunken duck. Sure, don't you remember last week when we slept on the shore of the mountain lake near the land of the Comyn clan. You snored so loudly that night, when we woke a dozen mallards had arrived — they thought they had found a long-lost cousin.'

Dúnán looked back over his shoulder, smiling. 'Well, at least we didn't have to go far to find breakfast.'

'True,' Cumhall laughed.

While Luchet rekindled the fire for breakfast, Muirne sat down with Cumhall.

'You've had that dream again, my love?'

'How do you know?' Cumhall asked.

'I can read it in your face. Was it the same?'

Since the night that Muirne had told him she was pregnant, Cumhall had been having the dream over and over. As the months moved forward the dream had continued to grow more vivid and more frightening as he became increasingly powerless to prevent his son from leaving him.

'Yes. Each time the child gets a little older. Each time he drifts further away. And it seems to be happening more often of late.'

'What of the horses?' Muirne probed.

'Yes, they're there again, getting closer too. And this time ...' Cumhall trailed off.

'This time what?' Muirne said, searching his face for answers.

'This time, I thought I could hear men's voices. I just wish I knew what it meant.'

'Well, whatever it means, I am sure that it is our son Demne you're seeing. What does he look like now?'

Cumhall beamed. 'He's beautiful. He has your eyes, and each time I see him, the likeness of you becomes clearer. He's fair of complexion and has the blondest of hair.'

'We will nickname him Fionn.' Muirne smiled as she uttered the Irish word for 'fair-haired'. As Luchet dished out breakfast with nettle tea, Cumhall continued to describe the vision of his son as best he could.

After their meal ended Muirne rose to speak. 'It's time,' she said. 'I will soon be welcoming this child into this world. I will have to settle in one place to have my baby safely.'

'Who will bring the baby into the world?' Cumhall asked. 'I don't think we can trust the midwives of the local clans to help deliver this baby safely without word getting back to Áed.'

Upon hearing this, Dúnán interrupted. 'My uncle Donncha has delivered many calves. He lives not a day's hike from here. I could go and ask him.'

'Thank you, Dúnán,' Muirne responded, 'and if I ever have a cow in labour, I will be sure to call on your uncle.' As Dúnán reddened, Muirne continued, 'There are only two people I can trust, if they are still out there. They were like mothers to me. Breac and Bodhmall. I have seen enough signs in nature to tell me they are still alive. Find them for me, Dúnán and Crimmal. My heart tells me that if they are still living you will find them deep in the midlands.'

A plan was agreed. Crimmal would search the central slopes of the Silvermine and Slieve Bloom Mountains while Dúnán would comb the bogs further north. Muirne, Cumhall and Luchet would make their way north and finally make a camp at Cnucha. There they would wait for the return of the men and, with luck, Breac and Bodhmall.

The Hill of Cnucha was in what would later become known as Dublin. Cumhall knew that it was near not only the High King's home of Tara but also Tadg's palace of Almu. 'Is making camp at Cnucha a good idea?' he asked Muirne.

'We've spent enough time in the south,' she began. 'With news that the Fianna are now regularly travelling north to keep a close eye on Scotland and other bands still being sent by Áed to search westwards, where stories speak of your clan now resting, I believe it is cleverer to stay under the window of those who would wish us harm. It is the last place they will expect to find us. Cnucha is difficult to attack and easy to defend, and it has good shelter.'

Over the next week, Muirne, Cumhall and Luchet travelled across the peaks of the Wicklow Mountains and into the lands below. Along the streams, ditches and dark paths they met few people. On the seventh evening, they arrived at the Hill of Cnucha and set up camp.

• • •

On the slope of Croghan Hill, Dúnán was snoring. He had explored the midland bogs surrounding this imposing hill but had not found Bodhmall and Breac. He hoped that Crimmal had had more luck. He set up camp and drifted off to sleep.

It just so happened that a small force of Áed's had drifted astray on their way to the Kingdom of Connacht. Dúnán's snores betrayed him. He woke, surrounded by half a dozen of Clan Morna. They swiftly bound and gagged him and started marching towards Almu, where Áed awaited their return.

• • •

Further south, in the Slieve Bloom Mountains, Crimmal indeed had more luck. It wasn't Áed's men but Muirne's foster mothers who crept up on him as he rested. He didn't have to explain much to convince the women. By daybreak they were well on their way to Cnucha.

This was just as well, for as soon as Dúnán's bruised body arrived at Almu, Tadg set to work. With the High King away in the north in the company of half of the Fianna, Tadg could be as merciless as he wanted in order to find out where Muirne and Cumhall were now hiding. Dúnán's name meant 'fortress', and true to this he withstood the thrashing and thumping of Áed and his men without talking. However, Tadg hadn't expected that the beatings would make Dúnán confess. He just wanted to exhaust him. For Tadg had the Dealra Dubh and his many books of sorcery to call upon. Alone in Almu's dungeon, he cast a powerful spell that put Dúnán into a deep stupor. Sapped of energy, Tadg's dark magic was too much, and he finally yielded.

Once Tadg had his information, he summoned Áed. 'Cnucha,' he announced. 'The Hill of Cnucha is where Muirne and Cumhall are and where we will exact our revenge. Go now, take your men, and don't return until there is no one on that hill left alive — including their child, Demne.'

• • •

At that very moment, Crimmal entered the camp on Cnucha with Bodhmall and Breac. As Muirne and the two old women were joyfully reunited, Cumhall and his brother exchanged a worried glance.

'No sign of Dúnán?' whispered Crimmal.

'No, not yet,' breathed Cumhall. 'But where he searched was closer to here.'

'Maybe he is just making sure that he has left no stone unturned.'

'It's a bog, Crimmal,' Cumhall replied. 'It shouldn't take him that long to turn over every stone. I'm afraid he has been captured. And if he has, I am worried that we may be at risk.'

• • •

'Father, don't leave me!'

Cumhall jumped from his bed and went to grab his sword and spear – but then hesitated. He knew he was still dreaming, but for the first time he seemed to recognise where he was. It was the Hill of Cnucha.

'Father, don't leave me!' Again, he heard the cry. Cumhall did not pick up his weapons. Instead, he turned to see the figure of an athletic young man with shoulder-length blond hair. As the young man began to fade away, Cumhall called to him.

'I am sorry, my son. I must leave you.' And for the very first time, the vision of his son did not continue to

41

fade, but instead sharpened. 'I must say goodbye to you, Demne.' His son came closer. Cumhall could see the man that he would grow to become. 'It is because I love you that I must let you go.' They were now standing face to face, so close that Cumhall could finally see the colour of his son's eyes, the contours of his cheeks and the rise of his nose. He truly was his mother's son.

They spoke at length. About the fears Demne had about leaving them. About the love Cumhall and Muirne already felt for their son. Cumhall reassured him that, although he might be on his own, he would never be truly alone. Never once did they hear the horses' hooves or men's voices. When Cumhall finally awoke he was not filled with fear but with peace. He felt happy and reassured. Dawn had not yet broken and only Luchet, who had been on watch, was awake. Cumhall now knew what the dreams meant, and he knew what he had to do. But first everyone needed to wake up.

• • •

Áed listened intently as his scouts described the hill and what they had seen. The steep hill was matted with impenetrable brambles. There was no way to reach the summit apart from a narrow path edged by huge rocks. Atop the hill was a small clearing covered in hawthorn trees, among which the scouts had spied a tent — and the figure of Cumhall.

Áed nodded. 'Difficult to attack and easy to defend. What I would expect from Cumhall. What about everyone else? What about Crimmal?'

'I didn't see him, but he could have been in the tent,' answered the scout.

'And Cumhall's treasure bag?'

'Yes, under his arm.'

Áed's hand gripped the enchanted holly spear tightly. 'We will attack this evening from the west, when the setting sun will blind them to our approach.'

• • •

Luchet was eating when he heard Cumhall shout for help. Cumhall thought that he spotted something, yet in the light of the low-lying western sun he couldn't be sure. He reached into his treasure bag and pulled out a Galician slingshot of the strongest leather and several stones and began firing into the thickets of gorse. On his third shot he heard them. One of Áed's men had been struck and cried out in pain. With their cover now revealed, a full attack began. Cumhall managed to severely injure several men as they charged forward along the narrow trail before Luchet came to his aid. They then both drew their swords and the fight turned white-hot.

Although Cumhall and Luchet were wildly outnumbered, the narrow path meant that only two enemies could approach at a time. From sunset into the darkness of night the battle raged on as both men held their ground. At times it looked like both Cumhall and Luchet were about to be overwhelmed but they managed to hold out and force their opponents to either retreat injured or die fighting.

As the last glimpses of light disappeared, Áed, who had remained in the shadows waiting for Cumhall to tire, came forward. In the near-darkness, Cumhall spotted him — spear in hand, preparing to unleash. Cumhall barely had time to pull a shield from his treasure bag before the magical spear smashed into it with such force that it sent Cumhall backwards — and his oxter bag downhill. Áed now grabbed his chance, cutting through his men to bear down on Cumhall. He would surely have killed him had it not been for Luchet, who drove a lance at Áed with all his might and managed to pierce his left eye. Writhing in pain, Áed spun around and delivered a deadly blow into Luchet's midriff.

Half-blinded, Áed called his men to his aid before grabbing his enchanted spear and ordering a retreat, leaving Cumhall to attend to his dear friend Luchet, who was now gasping for breath.

'You'll be okay,' Cumhall told him. 'A scratch, no more than that. We will be back around a campfire enjoying your leathery mutton stew in no time.'

'Yes,' Luchet replied, smiling weakly, 'but not in this world. In the meantime, you'll have to learn to cook for yourself, my friend.'

Although he was close to tears, Cumhall still managed to smile. And as he did, Luchet passed away in his arms from this world to the next.

• • •

At first light Áed's forces regrouped, ready to begin their terrible onslaught once again. As they approached, Cumhall saw Áed's wounded left eye had been bandaged. Cumhall lifted his sword in defiance and called out, 'Come at me, Goll, so I can finish the job my friend has started.' Áed bristled at the name by which he was to be known from that day forth — Goll meant 'one-eyed'. He knew that if he took on Cumhall in single combat he would be vanquished. So once again he fell back, and his men attempted to wear down Cumhall's strength.

By noon, with more than a dozen of his men now dead, Goll knew it was time. With his enchanted spear in hand, he marched forward until he stood face to face with his arch-rival. Tired, bloodied and exhausted,

Cumhall looked his enemy in the eye. 'You took your time confronting me.'

Goll just smirked and retorted, 'If you don't mind, I will take a little longer.' Goll looked down at the feet of Cumhall, who followed his stare. But it was not quick enough. Luachra, an evil, devious and bloodthirsty warrior had lain unnoticed among the dead since before dawn. And before Cumhall could react, Luachra rose and plunged a cruel dagger into his side. Cumhall grabbed Luachra by the throat but he could feel a fierce heat shooting through his side. Cumhall dropped to his knees.

Standing over Cumhall, Goll smiled a wicked smile. As Goll admired his enchanted spear's jewel-encrusted shaft glistening in the midday sun, Cumhall very slowly rose to his feet. He knew he was conquered – but he would not die on his knees.

As Goll thrust the spear through his heart, Cumhall let out a final cry for his friends, his wife and his unborn son. At the moment that Cumhall left this world, in a valley nearby, under the watchful eyes of Bodhmall and Breac, Demne entered it.

• • •

Crimmal looked anxiously at the Hill of Cnucha in the distance. The wind had carried the screams and shouts.

Crimmal could have sworn he heard the cry of his dear brother Cumhall just as Demne was born.

Two nights before, his brother had decided to move Muirne to a more exposed area, a day's travel from Cnucha. After all, Áed knew that Cumhall would protect his wife unto death. And Cumhall did — by leaving her in the care of his brother. And that is why he had had to let his son go, just like in the dream. It was the only way to save him.

• • •

'What do you mean, you don't know where my daughter has gone?' shouted Tadg.

'When we entered their tent, there was no one there. It was as if they had vanished!' Goll answered feebly.

'Are you sure they were ever there at all?' Tadg roared, unable to hold back his anger.

'I don't know. We searched for days afterwards but there was no sign of them. But we've killed Cumhall and Luchet, and we have Cumhall's treasure bag.'

'I know, you've already told me, but my awful, unruly, disobedient wretch of a daughter has got away once again!'

A commanding voice rang across the room. 'No, she hasn't.'

Tadg spun around to see Conn of the Hundred Battles. 'My lord,' Tadg said, bowing. 'I did not know you were returning so soon.'

'I know,' Conn answered drily. 'I guess that would explain why you have not yet got rid of Dúnán, who my men have just found tortured to death in your dungeon. But to answer your question, Chief Druid, your daughter Muirne is with me. She is currently recovering in Tara, being cared for by many of my best druids. I am aware of what you have done. Cumhall is dead. You have had your revenge, so now it ends.'

'And what of my daughter? When will you return her?' Tadg asked.

'I won't,' Conn replied sternly. 'She was left on the steps of my court a few days ago, gravely ill and needing care. Thankfully, she is now recovering, but she has suffered enough. She nearly lost her life. She lost her husband. And now she has lost her child.'

'Her child?' Tadg uttered in shock before demanding, 'How do you know the child is dead?'

'I don't. All I care for is her health. I realise I was wrong to have made Cumhall an outlaw and this is a mistake I must live with. But I will not make the same mistake with Muirne, so I have granted her refuge in Tara. She may reside there for as long as she wishes. She is not to be harmed ever again.' He paused. 'Tadg, you are no longer Chief Druid. Our faith in you has been lost.'

The High King withdrew, leaving Tadg alone with his thoughts and his anger. He knew that one day he would have his revenge.

• • •

The blond tufts of hair of a little baby poked out from a cloth sling. The sling was attached to Bodhmall, who paced slowly behind Breac. The cheerful gurgles of the baby were their only source of happiness.

Muirne had been able to spend just two nights with her baby before she became so ill that there was no other choice but for Crimmal to bring her to Tara. The druids there were the only ones who could save her. In a whisper, she had instructed Breac and Bodhmall to call the newborn 'Fionn', after his golden hair. He would always be Demne to her, but she hoped that this name would protect his identity, for a little while at least. Before he headed westwards for his own safety, Crimmal bade farewell to little Fionn, who was now on his way to his new fosters mothers' hidden home high on Slieve Bloom.

THE THREE BLIND SMITHS

'H e's late,' Bodhmall murmured. She tasted the fine hare stew that Breac had prepared.

'He's always late,' Breac said, smiling. 'We'll just have to leave him some.'

Close by, in the shadow of Slieve Bloom, a boy lay silently atop a pile of damp moss. In the half-light that shone weakly through the dense oak branches he was barely visible. A young hare, now only a few feet away from his grasp, was calmly nibbling the few shoots of grass that sprouted towards the uncertain sun. Nibbling ... nibbling ... WHOOOSH!

A moment later the hare was in his grasp. Frozen. Looking down, the boy grinned. 'You need to become

51

faster, little hare, just as I need to get home and eat food so I can become faster still. But be warned — I'll be back.' He lay the little ball of shivering fur down and took off towards home.

• • •

'So great of you to find the time to join us, young Fionn,' Bodhmall greeted him as she ended her meal.

Looking up from beneath a great mop of blond hair, Fionn smiled sheepishly. 'Sorry, Bodhmall,' he replied and then sat down and began to eat.

Bodhmall coughed.

'And sorry, Breac. The stew tastes lovely,' Fionn hastily added.

Usually their dinners were full of chat as Fionn told his foster parents about his exploits of the day — how far he had travelled, what he had climbed, where he had swum and what animals he had caught, spoken to or hunted. Bodhmall and Breac, who were both said to be almost seventy but looked twenty years younger, would listen intently, throwing in an occasional question or an instruction for Fionn to slow down. This evening, however, the atmosphere was different. When Fionn began to tell them about his day, it became clear that Bodhmall's mind was somewhere else, and so too was

Breac's. Fionn ate in silence as the women drank their nettle tea and looked at the distant stars.

As he was finishing his meal, Bodhmall's voice punctured the silence. 'Fionn, since you were an infant, Breac and I have cared for you as if you were our own son.' Bodhmall stopped and glanced at Breac, who looked away. 'However, we have taught you as much as we can of the wild ways. You will soon have to leave.'

'What? To where? With who?' Fionn protested loudly. 'There is still much that you can teach me and that I want to learn.'

Her eyes growing glassy, Bodhmall continued. 'Fionn, we are hunters, trackers and warriors, but there is very little we can still teach you.' Deep down, Fionn knew she was right. When it came to tracking and hunting, few animals could outfox him. He had been taught to spot a spider in a rainstorm and a dandelion seed in a gale. His sense of smell was so strong that he could pinpoint a wood mouse hiding in a grove of purple stinkhorns. He could outstrip a hare over open ground, and over rugged ground he was quicker than a mountain deer. With one stone from his sling he could make a duck drop from the sky.

Despite this knowledge, Fionn did not want to leave. Slieve Bloom was the only home he knew, and the thoughts of leaving frightened him. 'What if I don't want to go?' he asked. 'What if I want to stay and live here with you? You are my family, and this is my home.'

'This is not your home, Fionn,' Bodhmall answered sternly. 'It is in Tara, which all true Fianna champions call home, and you know that. However, I am afraid that even if you wanted to stay you do not have a choice. We have heard the wrens whispering. They say that your mortal enemy Goll Mac Morna has heard of a young boy with blond hair hunting at the fringes of this forest. He guessed that it was you, Fionn, son of Cumhall, and the weasels have confirmed your identity to his men. They are coming for you, Fionn.'

It had been Bodhmall's greatest fear. The Mac Mornas were legendary for their tracking. Although she and Breac had their allies in the woods and the wilds, so too did Goll. Were the Mac Mornas to arrive, it would only be a matter of time before they would find Fionn. Both Bodhmall and Breac were prepared to fight to the death to keep their promise to his mother. But they knew that they could not hold out against the forces of Goll Mac Morna — they would be defeated and Fionn would be slain.

'When will I need to leave?' Fionn asked.

'The day after tomorrow,' said Bodhmall. 'Three blind smiths will arrive here tomorrow evening. Their names are Gobán the Short, Garb the Stubby and Gadra the Tall. They have been making spears, swords, axes and arrowheads for us for years. We haven't seen them in quite some time, but they are currently travelling down the Shannon to bring us new weapons and to sharpen our blades. Tomorrow evening they will visit us, and when they leave you will leave with them.'

Breac looked at a dejected Fionn and whispered, 'Come on now, Fionn, it could be worse. It could be raining. Pull out the brandubh board and let's play a few games. Maybe losing a few rounds to me will make you feel better.' She elbowed him playfully. Brandubh was a traditional Celtic game — more chess than checkers — and Fionn had never managed to beat Breac. But that night was special, so she only beat him by a small amount.

The next morning, Fionn awoke to one of Breac's most delicious breakfasts of wild morel mushrooms and hazelnuts. He then went with Bodhmall on one final hunting trip. Having spotted the fresh hoofprints of a young stag, Fionn looped around a small mountain peak to where he guessed it would be grazing, while Bodhmall followed its trail.

As he made his way around the mountain's western face, Fionn heard raised voices. He stopped to figure out where they came from and then slowly approached what sounded like an argument. He hid behind a bush and listened.

'What do you mean, you forgot my tongs?'

'I put it in last night before we set off.'

'Well then, how could it not be there now? Feel around for it some more.'

'I have been feeling around for it for the last half-hour. It's not there. You'll just have to use my tongs.'

From where he crouched, Fionn could see the blind smiths whom Bodhmall had spoken about.

'Your tongs!' the short one snapped. 'I'll have you know the weapons I make are pieces of art. If I use your useless tongs, they'll be pieces of comedy!'

'Comedy!' the tall one replied incredulously. 'Well, we'll see just how funny my tongs are when I shove them up your —'

'Shush!' went the stubby one, who had up to this point remained quiet as his friends bickered. He addressed the bush that Fionn was hiding behind. 'So, you must be the boy they call Fionn?'

Fionn was shocked at having been noticed.

'What? You thought you could creep up on us because we are blind? Did Bodhmall and Breac not teach you never to hunt upwind from your prey in case they smell you coming? Especially when you smell like a sweaty teenager?'

'I don't smell — ow!' Fionn yelped as the shortest of the smiths caught him square in the face with a small pebble. 'That hurt!' he said, rubbing the spot where he had been so skilfully hit.

'Upwind and loud,' chuckled the smith. 'We will definitely have to have words with your foster parents.'

But before Fionn could respond, he heard a familiar voice. 'Well, you might as well start now.'

'Bodhmall, my old friend,' Gadra, the tallest smith, replied. Within minutes, the four were chatting warmly as only old friends can.

• • •

As they tucked into their evening stew, it was Gobán the Short who spoke first. 'In all the years we've visited you we've never brought you so many pieces of work.'

'We just thought we'd do a bit of redecorating, perhaps build an extension.'

'Come on now, Breac,' Garb said. 'You're really going to redecorate using daggers, blades, arrowheads and axes? We've known each other for too long now to start holding on to secrets. Are you expecting a war?'

'We're not keeping a secret,' Bodhmall cut in. 'We just thought we'd wait until after dessert to ask you to risk your lives for this young boy.'

'Well, if it's all the same to you,' Gobán said, 'I'm happy to hear this now.'

So Bodhmall explained who Fionn was, why he was in danger and how the Mac Mornas were on their way. 'And that is why we need you to bring him to safety while there is still time. Will you help us?'

'I'll help myself to dessert,' Garb interrupted. 'As for the boy, does he cook? Because if he does, we could do with one to come with us.'

The night continued with humour and banter as they filled each other in on what had happened since they had last met. Breac even told them the only smith joke she knew.

'Did you hear that Bodhmall got a dog from a smith last month?' she said, hardly able to hold in her chuckling. 'But when they came home, he made a bolt for the door!'

The whole group fell around laughing except for Fionn, who couldn't remember any dog.

• • •

The next morning, Fionn and the blind smiths left before the sun had risen. A few days later, as Bodhmall and Breac had guessed, Goll arrived. By then, however, the camp was deserted. And when Goll's men did pick up tracks, they were the footsteps of Bodhmall and Breac, which led them eastwards until the prints mysteriously disappeared. By the time Goll had realised he had been tricked, Fionn and the smiths were more than a week away and still marching westwards.

• • •

'I'm afraid we are terrible cooks.'

'We can never figure out the right amount of butter.'

'We're always adding salt when we should be adding honey.'

'We start with a dessert and finish with a soup.'

'So it's a good thing you came along to cook for us, Fionn.'

And with that, all three smiths started laughing. But Fionn didn't mind doing the cooking. He would rather prepare some decent food himself than eat the tasteless food that the smiths cooked. However, what Fionn did mind was that he was now bald! While Fionn didn't know who exactly was responsible, what he did know was that someone had cut all his hair as he slept during the very first night. There was, of course, a reason for his desperate appearance. Across the midlands most people had now heard of Goll Mac Morna's search for a young boy with bright blond hair. It was safer for Fionn to be passed off as a young bald apprentice to three old blind smiths.

As the days passed, Fionn got used to his shaven head. As they slowly made their way west, despite the haircut and having to cook for three old bickering men who rarely said thanks, Fionn grew to like the trio. Indeed, Fionn had persuaded them to show him the basic skills of metalwork in return for his cooking. Fionn was a quick learner, and he moved quickly from sharpening to shaping and then from designing to moulding. After a month, he made a dagger of some quality that fitted neatly along the inside of his wrist.

• • •

Late one evening after a particularly enjoyable meal, Fionn asked how they knew his foster mothers. He was met with silence and it seemed that Fionn might have offended them, but, before he could apologise, Gobán told him the sorry tale of the Smiths of River Shannon.

'Almost a half-century ago,' he began, 'we worked south of where the great River Shannon opens up on its way out to sea. We were brothers and blacksmiths, like our widowed father and his forefathers before. We used to make swords and ploughs for the local warriors and farmers. But in our spare time, despite the disapproval of our father, we would try to out-do each other in making jewellery, each piece finer than the last.

'Eventually, word of our work spread to Rígán, an evil lord who lived on the river island of Inis Sibhtonn. One night, on our way back from a local feast, his warriors captured us. We were ordered to make him a piece of jewellery so beautiful it would take his breath away. If we refused, he swore to have our father murdered in his bed. For weeks we shaped and moulded the gold and silver metals he brought us. Finally, after a full season of toil, we had made the most amazing brooch of silver, enamel and gold filigree that the world has ever seen.'

'Did he keep his word and let you go?' Fionn asked.

'Yes,' Gadra said solemnly. 'He did let us go, but he made sure we would never make a piece of jewellery as beautiful ever again. He blinded us and then murdered our father.'

'We were turned out into the wild, left to fend for ourselves,' Garb continued, 'and soon we were left cold, hungry and not far from death's door.'

'What about the High King and the Fianna?' Fionn asked angrily.

'This was nearly fifty years before the time of Conn of the Hundred Battles,' Garb continued. 'There was no High King who controlled the whole country, and the Fianna fought for whichever nobleman gave them shelter during winter. It was a dark time in our history.'

'But into that darkness,' Gobán spoke, 'entered Bodhmall and Breac. They found us lost, alone and starving, and took us in. They were just like us: exiled from their home.'

'Exiled?' Fionn asked. In all the time with the two women, he had always thought that they hid in order to protect him.

'Yes, exiled,' Gobán said. 'You see, Bodhmall and Breac grew up in the same settlement. They played together as kids and soon became inseparable. When they both approached the age of eighteen, just like your mother Muirne had been, they were told that they were each to marry a man they had never met. But just like your mother, they were already in love. Not with a member of the Fianna — but with each other. Determined not to be separated and knowing their parents would never accept their love, they were left with no choice but to escape together. And in doing so they became exiles.'

Gadra now took over. 'But they had not allowed that to destroy them, and they made us realise that we couldn't let our blindness decide our future. And they didn't stop there. The night they heard what had been done to us, and to our father, they left us and did not come back until the following morning with the brooch and a pouch of silver and gold pieces. They gave us all of this, helped us set up again as smiths and asked us if we could supply them with weapons every few years, which we did for decades, until requests from them fell silent more than ten years ago.'

'What of Rígán?' Fionn asked.

'We don't know. We know he disappeared that night and was never found,' Gobán said. 'So I guess that brooch really did take his breath away.'

• • •

After a few weeks of slow, steady travel, the group crossed the Shannon, not far from where it greeted the sea. They had met very few people as they travelled the lesser-known routes, and it was beginning to look like they had escaped the grip of Goll and his men. Fionn had started to think about his freedom (and his hair finally growing back). One day, he was returning triumphantly to the camp with a young hare and some wild leeks when he heard raised voices. When he crept closer, he could see that a band of thieves were threatening the smiths.

'Where do you keep the rest of it?' a bandit with a crescent-shaped scar that reached from his chin to his eye said menacingly.

'Keep what?' Gadra innocently replied.

SMACK! The ruffian struck Gadra across the face, knocking him to the floor. 'The gold and silver! You are smiths and you make precious things. And those precious things you make, make money.'

'Oh, you must have us mixed up, my friend,' Gadra said, rubbing his chin as he rose to his knees. 'We work for food and shelter — not for gold and silver.'

SMACK! The thief's fist smashed into Gadra's face and sent him back down. From where Fionn hid he could also see the bloodied faces of Garb and Gobán. Both had their hands bound behind their backs. They had obviously been asked the same set of questions and had given the same wrong replies.

Fionn's temper grew at the sight of his new friends' misfortune. He readied his throwing spear, unsheathed his hunting blade and stepped forward. Unfortunately, what he didn't know was that this was no ordinary band of robbers. It was a group led by Beirgín the Wicked, a colossus of a man who was said to have Fomorian blood in him. The Fomorians were supernatural beings who had been the enemies of the first Irish settlers. They had been driven out of Ireland, but it was said that their blood still flowed in a few men and women, giving them magical powers. One of these men was Beirgín, who had the strength of five men and was as fast as the western wind.

As the cruel ruffian with the scar threw up his hand to strike Gadra again, Fionn lunged forward. His spear struck the man with such force that he was dead before he hit the ground. Drawing his sword, Fionn then turned to the thieves who were guarding the smiths and struck them down in quick succession. Then, as Fionn spun round to face the rest of the bandits — BANG — everything went black.

• • •

In the spring, swans migrate west. It is said that they only fly east during this time when they need to share bad news. When Bodhmall and Breac saw their white-feathered friends approach them one evening several weeks after they had said goodbye to their foster son, they knew it could only mean one thing — bad news. Their fears were soon confirmed. The swans told them that Fionn had been caught by Beirgín the Wicked and that the three blind smiths had been killed.

The smiths had not told Beirgín who the boy was, so Fionn was safe. At least for now. However, Beirgín was on his way to meet Goll Mac Morna to sell him some of what he had stolen from the smiths. Of course, the prices at which Beirgín sold his loot to Goll were always low. After all, he couldn't charge the man who allowed him to rob and steal so freely a very high price. However, Fionn knew it would not take long for Mac Morna to work out that this bald and bruised boy with Beirgín was Fionn Mac Cumhaill, son of his arch-enemy — and the child he wanted to kill!

Both Breac and Bodhmall knew that they didn't have any time to grieve for their three old friends. They packed some of their best weapons and took off. Time was ticking.

• • •

Fionn awoke in darkness with a groggy, throbbing head. He could taste the dried blood on his lips. He tried to move and stretch, but found he was tied up in a sack. Despite being curled in a ball, with his toes bound to his fingers, his ankles to his elbows and his legs around his ears, Fionn knew he had to think — and think quick — because Goll would not let him live more than a minute once he realised who he really was.

Suddenly, he felt the full force of a stick bang into him. 'Urghhh,' he groaned.

Beirgín laughed. 'The little warrior has woken up. Little warrior, you killed five of my best men. Okay, two of them were only good for eating crubeens and robbing old women, but even still, nobody attacks Beirgín the Wicked and gets away with it.' He gave Fionn another painful dig. 'Struggle all you want, little warrior. I have bound you with a hundred knots. And tomorrow I will sell you to Goll Mac Morna, who will pay me a handsome sum for a little warrior boy his men can practise on.'

• • •

After a full day on horseback, Beirgín and his men were only a few hours from Tara when a dense drizzle set in that quickly turned to pouring rain. As it was almost dark, Beirgín declared they would set up camp in a grove of elder trees. He sent one of his men onwards in the driving rain to tell Goll that they would soon arrive.

They sat down to eat. Beirgín opened the sack and allowed Fionn's head out so he could drink half a cup of water. Fionn could finally see who had knocked him out with such unnatural speed and strength. Beirgín must have been seven feet tall, with wide eyes and a wild beard that contained food he had eaten more than a week ago. Around the campfire were six other bandits, each as ugly and menacing as the last. Fionn did not know what had happened to the three smiths, but he suspected the worst. When he saw Garb's favourite hammer poking out of one of the bags upon which Beirgín now sat, he knew deep down that his friends had been killed.

As Beirgín stripped meat off the leg of a wild boar, he started to tease Fionn. 'So, little warrior, you thought you could defeat Beirgín the Wicked? Did your parents never teach you that Beirgín the Wicked has Fomorian blood in him? And that he is stronger than five men and faster than the western wind? There was never a chance of you hurting a hair on my chin, let alone defeating me.'

It was then that Fionn had an idea. Of course his parents had never told him about the Fomorians. He never knew them, so how could they have? But Bodhmall and Breac had spoken of them. They were supernaturally strong and fast and impossible to defeat in battle — but they could also be rather ... stupid.

'I am sorry to have offended you, Beirgín,' Fionn said. 'Had I known you had Fomorian blood in you, I would never have attacked you.'

'What?' Beirgín asked. 'You think you can apologise and I will just let you go?'

'Oh no!' Fionn interrupted. 'I would never expect you to release me. Not after what I did. I just wanted to say that those three old men had warned me about you.'

Although suspicious, Beirgín was intrigued. He commanded Fionn to continue.

'They told me all about the Fomorians. That they were so strong they simply flattened mountains with their hands. That they were so quick that shooting stars couldn't keep up with them. That they were so handsome that even their reflections fell in love with them. And that they were so tough that they didn't hammer nails, they just told them where to go.'

At this stage Beirgín couldn't hide his pride and satisfaction, and he was beaming from ear to ear. He was just about to lie back and take another drink from the jug of wine he held when Fionn added, 'And it is because of your strength, your speed, your fearsomeness and your toughness that I feel so embarrassed that I dared to attack your men yesterday. You are truly the greatest warrior I have met.'

'Indeed,' said Beirgín, glowing.

'It just shows what you can become, even if you're not very smart.'

'WHAT?' roared Beirgín.

'Oh, I didn't mean to upset you. In fact, I disagreed with the three smiths. I said that I thought the Fomorians sounded very intelligent. But the smiths told me that they were thicker than jam and that they wouldn't even be able to answer a simple children's riddle!'

'What riddle?' bellowed Beirgín, now towering over Fionn, with one hand on his enormous axe.

'I'm sorry I brought it up. I told them you all sounded very intelligent, so let's just forget about it and get some sleep. We have an early start in the morning.'

But as Fionn lowered his head back down into the sack, Beirgín grabbed him by the neck. 'The riddle, boy! Ask me the riddle!'

'If you insist,' replied Fionn, 'but you will laugh when you hear it. It's so very easy. Okay, here goes — what is harmless but can kill you?'

Beirgín's face went blank. For minutes he sat still staring into the distance as he tried searching the empty rooms of his head for an answer.

'A sword?'

'No,' answered Fionn.

'Of course. It's not a sword. I meant a ... er ... knife.'

'No, not a knife.'

'An axe, then?'

The more guesses he made, the angrier Beirgín got. Knowing what he was like when he got angry, his band of robbers sneaked away. Beirgín kept looking for a solution, and Fionn kept telling him his answers were wrong. However, as he listened to Beirgín's hare-brained answers, Fionn was unpicking the knots he was tied up with, one by one by one.

'A horse?'

'No.'

'How about a loaf of bread?'

'No.'

'A baby?'

'No.'

'A cough?'

'No.'

'A breeze? A fart? Indigestion?'

'No. No. No.'

On and on Beirgín went. A few hours before dawn, he finally fell into a deep slumber. As he snored, Fionn continued to unknot.

• • •

The next morning, Beirgín's group of bandits awoke to see their leader still sleeping. Not wanting to be the one to rouse him, they decided to make the most of the morning off and have a lie-in. Meanwhile, Fionn kept untying. By noon he was nearly free. Which was just as well, because just then Beirgín was waking up. As Fionn was loosening the last of the knots, Beirgín yawned and stood up. Looking around at his men, who were still sleeping, he realised how late it was. He gave one of them a kick up the backside so hard that it sent the bandit into the nearby bushes. This woke the rest of them. Beirgín then regarded the sack that held Fionn. He took his hazel stick and gave the sack a heavy prod.

'Wake up, little warrior. We are late for Goll Mac Morna because of your riddle. Tell me what the answer is so that I can be done with you.'

Fionn didn't answer. Beirgín prodded him again, and Fionn let out a grunt. But again he didn't answer. The third time Beirgín prodded him, Fionn muttered something under his breath, but Beirgín couldn't hear him.

'What?' snarled Beirgín. 'What did you say?'

Another mumble from inside the sack.

'Wait. Let me open this sack so I can hear you properly.'

And just as he was opening the sack, Fionn finished untying the last knot. As the ruffian looked in, Fionn swiftly stabbed his left eye with an index finger. Beirgín clapped his hand to his eye and staggered back in surprise.

'ARGHHH!' he roared. 'My eye! Get him!'

But by this stage Fionn had jumped out of the sack and grabbed Garb's hammer. He had the upper hand on Beirgín's band of surprised thieves. Fionn swiftly knocked them out, knocked them down and knocked them over. Then he turned to Beirgín, who, despite only having sight in one eye, looked as ferocious as ever.

'You think you will still defeat me, little warrior? I will kill you just as I killed your friends and I will send you to Goll Mac Morna in little pieces. You cannot defeat the blood of the Fomorians!'

But Fionn was grinning from ear to ear. He calmly repeated his riddle. 'What is harmless but can kill you?'

'Tell me before I silence you forever!' roared Beirgín.

'Time,' Fionn answered with a smile.

As he smiled, he looked over Beirgín's shoulder into the faces of his foster parents, who had come to his aid just in time – and who were now advancing towards Beirgín with their weapons raised.

• • •

When it was all over and Beirgín was slain, Bodhmall and Breac embraced Fionn.

'We are sorry, child,' Bodhmall whispered softly.

'I am sorry, too — for your friends,' Fionn said.

'Don't worry, the blame lies only with Beirgín, whom we have now killed, and with Goll Mac Morna. But I am afraid you must escape again, this time on your own. You are ready. Goll Mac Morna will soon hear what has happened under his very nose and he will come after you like never before.'

'What will I do?' Fionn asked.

'Be like the mist,' Breac answered. 'Move from mountain to marsh, from sea to stream, not staying too long in any one place so that your scent is as slight as a primrose within a wild meadow. And keep away from others, at least for a while. While Tadg and his magic might be waning, Goll will search every clachan and village. Only the bravest will resist giving you up to him.'

'And what of you?' he wondered aloud.

'We will stay here. Like the smiths, we are close to the end of our days. We can no longer move from place to place, living in exile. Instead, we will return home to Slieve Bloom and see out the future together.'

Fionn knew that he could not change their minds, so he gave them a final hug and set off northwards to Ulster. When he looked back for the last time, they were holding hands and waving to him. And that was the last image he ever had of them.

THE HURLERS OF DONARD

As Fionn gazed into the bright amber flames of his campfire, the words of Bodhmall came back to him. 'There are three things that give great comfort in this life, Fionn — watching a fire burn, watching waves wash in and out and spending time in the company of others.'

In the year and a half since he had bid Bodhmall and Breac farewell, Fionn had watched many fires burn and countless waves wash in and out. After narrowly avoiding capture by Beirgín, he had made his way north. He had spent the summer through to autumn, including his thirteenth birthday, high in the Sperrin Mountains, where few people lived. In winter, the bushes grew bare and game left the peaks to take shelter from the harsh northern winds, so he spent the cold months hunting, fishing and foraging near the great Lough Neagh. The spring had brought brightness and warmth, but it had also brought people outdoors. So once again he moved, eastwards this time, to the Mourne Mountains.

Throughout this time all he had for company were wild animals. And although they offered him some solace, he missed the companionship of others, especially Bodhmall and Breac. So, at the beginning of that second summer on the run, as shouts, roars and cries of joy drifted up from the valley below, Fionn found himself drawn back to the world of mortals.

• • •

It had taken him a few days before he realised that they weren't fighting each other. Instead they were playing some sort of sport. Fionn crept down the mountain slope through the furze bushes until he could command a view of the field. Each evening, boys his own age would gather there. Holding strangely shaped sticks, they would chase after a small ball. They would hit it either one way or the other, depending on the colour of their tunics. That was as much sense as he could make of it.

78

Up and down they went waving sticks and shouting. Along the sides of the field, a line of animated spectators cheered them on. At first it looked violent. But as each game passed, Fionn realised that much fun was being had. And with every roar of approval, the more Fionn wanted to get involved. But how?

'Aaaaarghhhhhh!'

Fionn's thoughts were interrupted by a shout from one of the players below. Looking down, he could see the red-haired youth who had dominated proceedings holding his ankle and writhing in pain. Clashes were common, and rarely an evening passed without at least one person getting a little bloodied or bruised. However, judging from the worried faces that now surrounded the youth, this injury looked a lot more serious. With the game having reached a premature end, Fionn decided he would use the opportunity to slip unnoticed up the mountain. Or so he thought.

• • •

There it was again. A flash of fair hair. Hardly visible. But it was definitely there. Cana had become suspicious that the young hurlers of Clan Rooney were being watched as they played in the shadow of Slieve Donard. She had kept a close eye on the surrounding hills. Finally, after a wonder strike from her red-haired elder brother Iollan, she had again spotted the slightest flicker of activity among the furze bushes.

The next day, she again saw movement in the same thicket of shrubs. Someone was watching. And that someone, Cana thought, could only be the opposition! They had obviously come to spy on the boys ahead of the great Ulster hurling championship. Every summer, the young boys of the province followed in the footsteps of their forefathers by playing epic games against each other. These games would begin in the late afternoon, often with the first call of the evening corncrake, and continue until the last sliver of sun set over the horizon. The games would be played all summer long until just two sides were left to fight it out at the home of hurling — the ancient fort of Emain Macha. The champions would win the right to bring the great black bull of Aughnacloy back to their clan for a whole year.

Cana, not yet fourteen, was small and nimble, with long brown hair that she was always tucking behind her ear. She was brave to a fault and dreamed of bringing the bull home to her family but knew it was unlikely to ever happen. Girls rarely played hurling. Not because they couldn't, but because most captains were boys and many of them wouldn't play on the same team as girls. Cana could not remember a girl ever playing for Clan

Rooney. With her brother now captain she couldn't imagine that changing. He wouldn't even allow her to train with the team, even though she could run rings around most of them!

Despite all that, it didn't stop her wanting the team to win. They represented her clan and her village after all. And with her brother Iollan in great form, Cana thought this year might be their year – the year that they would finally beat their fierce rivals, Clan Colgan of Annaclone. She did not want anything to threaten that, least of all a spy, so that was why for this training session she was not standing on the sidelines but slowly snaking her way across the mountainside towards that mop of fair hair. Fifty steps away. Thirty steps away. Ten steps away.

'Aaaaarghhhhhh!'

Cana's attention was diverted to the playing field. There, in the centre of the field, her brother lay writhing in pain, holding his ankle. As she gazed with worry down at Iollan, she briefly forgot the person she had been stalking. And when she looked back, the mop of fair hair was gone. At least for the moment.

• • •

In near darkness, Fionn sneaked into the village. With one player now injured, he thought the opportunity for him to join in might have arrived. But first he needed to learn how to play the game, and to do that he needed a stick. All his attempts at making one had failed miserably. So, he was going to take one. After just a few minutes' searching, he found several sticks lying up against the wall of a small hut.

Quickly, he grabbed the most worn one. Perhaps its owner would appreciate having to find a replacement. However, as he turned to leave, Cana stepped out in front of him.

'Care to tell me where you're going with that?'

'With what?' Fionn responded, shocked at her sudden appearance.

'The hurl.'

'The what?'

'The hurl you're holding,' Cana repeated, as if she was speaking to a Fomorian.

'You mean the stick?'

'Yes, the stick,' she said sarcastically. 'The hurley stick!'

'Oh, I didn't know that's what it's called.'

'Come on now!' Cana snapped. 'You want me to believe that a spy from the opposition doesn't know what a hurl is?'

'I'm not a spy,' Fionn replied, hurt by the accusation.

'Well, what are you then? Sneaking around at night

stealing our hurls? Spending the evenings watching the boys train?'

Fionn was taken aback. As careful as he had been, she must have noticed him watching from the furze.

'I'm not a spy. I'm a ... em ... shepherd,' he blurted out.

'A shepherd, eh?' Cana said. 'Really? With what clan?'

'I don't have one.'

'Oh, so whose sheep are you shepherding?'

'I don't know,' Fionn answered. 'I'm ... em ... freelance?'

'What on earth is a freelance?'

'It's like when you sell your lance or sword to a chief to fight for them in exchange for food and shelter. You become a freelance. I do the same, except for sheep.'

'You fight for sheep?' Cana giggled.

'No, I sell my lance to work and protect the sheep.'

'And are there big wolves up on those slopes?' Cana asked, taking stock of Fionn's lance, sword, dagger and hand-axe.

Fionn knew that, whoever this girl was, she didn't seem to believe him. He also knew that she could raise an alarm before he would have a chance to do anything. Presuming he would be able to do something. The way she was holding her own hurley stick suggested that he might have his work cut out.

'Yes, lots of wolves. It's always dangerous.'

Having pushed him so far, Cana relented and turned the conversation back to the hurl. 'Why are you sneaking around at night robbing hurls when you could just come down and join in with the boys?'

'I'm not very good, and I don't have a proper hurl. And I ... em ... didn't want to embarrass myself.'

After some thought, Cana smiled. 'Fine. I'll tell you what, on the far side of the mountain, there are three ginormous boulders surrounded by heather. Meet me there tomorrow after the hurling is over and before it's dark. We'll make you a hurl and I'll teach you how to play.'

'Thanks,' Fionn replied. 'But why? Why help me?'

'It'll give me someone to practise with,' Cana said. 'What's your name, by the way?'

After a brief hesitation, the reply came. 'Fionn. My friends call me Fionn. What's yours?'

'I'm Cana. It means "wolf cub", but don't worry, I don't bite — well, not my friends anyway.'

As Fionn left he wore a broad smile and felt a sense of satisfaction that had long been missing from his life.

• • •

True to her word, Cana met Fionn the following night.

'So, what did you make your hurl from?' she asked.

'Oak,' said Fionn sheepishly.

Cana could not contain her laughter. 'Well, that might explain why you've struggled. You can't just make a hurl out of any old wood. It must be the ash. Only ash has the right balance of strength and flexibility. But you don't find many ash trees in the Mournes.'

'So that's why we're down in the Glens,' said Fionn.

Having found a perfect ash specimen from which to make a hurl, they were soon ready to begin lessons.

'Lesson one,' Cana announced. 'Striking the sliotar.'

'The what?' Fionn interrupted.

'The sliotar. We call the ball a sliotar. Let's see how you strike it.'

Cana showed him how to strike the ball against the smooth face of a granite rock wall so that it would return to him. This skill Fionn quickly mastered, and soon every strike bounced back to him with growing ferocity, and which he caught with equal expertise.

'This is easier than I thought,' Fionn boasted.

'Well then, let's move to the next skill,' Cana answered. 'I want you to strike from your other side.'

With that, Fionn turned around.

'What are you doing?' Cana asked him.

'Striking from my other side.'

'That's not striking from your other side,' she said, chuckling. 'That's striking in the opposite direction. I want you to strike from your bad side. Like this.' Cana struck the sliotar backhand as accurately as she had struck it from her normal side.

Fionn's hurl whistled through the air as his first attempt saw the sliotar drop harmlessly to the ground — along with his smugness.

'Well, that's your first piece of homework,' Cana said. 'I want you to practise striking from your bad side.'

And that is how Fionn learned to play hurling. Every evening for a fortnight, Fionn would meet Cana and she would puck around with him. And every evening she would teach him a new skill and explain the rules as they practised. One evening she would show him how to tackle by blocking a ball and hooking a competitor's hurl to stop them from getting a shot away. Another evening it would be a lesson on holding the hurl so he could keep the sliotar balanced atop, as steady as a sessile oak, while he sprinted forward. In the silence and solitude of the mountain, Fionn would practise all day, only stopping to eat and to watch the boys train — all of whom he had come to know by name.

● ● ●

'We won't be able to train tomorrow,' Cana told Fionn.

'Why not?'

'Tomorrow is the first round of the annual championship,' she answered.

'Already?'

'Yes. We will play Clan Cernaich of Belleeks.'

'Do you think you will win?' Fionn asked.

'We should. Clan Cernaich are usually the worst team in the championship. But the injury to Iollan has left a hole in the team that has yet to be filled. The lads miss their captain and a new one has not yet been selected.'

'Why don't you play?' Fionn asked. 'You're as good a player as any of them.'

'Well, duh! Because I'm a girl, and the captain never picks girls and the others won't play alongside me. Why do you think I have been practising with you all this time?'

'Because I'm good craic to be around,' Fionn said with a grin. Remembering his old friends Bodhmall and Breac and how skilful, strong and proud they were, he added, 'It's a pretty stupid rule, isn't it?'

'I know,' Cana replied glumly.

• • •

The following day, Fionn took his usual spot in the furze and watched as Clan Rooney, the hurlers of Donard, did battle with Clan Cernaich. It was a tight, nervous affair that had few traces of skill or style. In the end, after a late pair of strikes from the Aonghusa brothers upfront, Clan Rooney squeezed out the narrowest of victories. The next day, a subdued Cana arrived to train with Fionn.

'Close game,' he said.

'Too close,' Cana responded, 'and probably the only win we'll see this year.'

'When is the next match?'

'Next week we travel to Garvaghy to play Clan Mahon.'

'And what are they like?'

'Better than us at the moment, anyway.'

• • •

The next day, Cana arrived at the boys' evening training to the sound of an argument.

'A freelance what?' shouted Barra at the visitor. Cana didn't immediately recognise who the team's fullback was speaking angrily to. But then she realised it was Fionn.

'A freelance hurler,' Fionn said to the angry-looking boys, who were all armed with hurls.

'A freelance hurler?' Iollan repeated. 'What the gods is that?'

'A freelance hurler,' Cana interrupted. 'Surely you've heard of freelance hurlers? They travel the country playing hurling for teams in return for food and a place to rest. Our arch-rivals Clan Lochlainn use them all the time, except their freelance hurlers are usually Fianna members who are over-age!'

'That's right,' Fionn added. 'Exactly what this girl said, except I'm not over-age. I am only just fourteen. I've travelled from south Munster to sell my skills, and all I ask for in return is food, water and a bed to sleep in.'

But Iollan was suspicious. The idea of someone not from Clan Rooney playing for the hurlers of Donard didn't appeal to him. However, Cana was right. Clan Lochlainn were sure to have their own players not from their clan. He knew his team needed someone good, or they were sure to go out in the next round.

'Okay, let's see how good you are. Go join Senán, Tadc, Rannal, Naoise, Martan, Fergal and Domnall over there and line up against the others.'

What happened next shocked everyone — except for Cana. Fionn weaved and dodged, blocked, hooked and struck the sliotar with such speed and precision that his team carved up the opposing side like butter. Iollan then decided to play Fionn alone against three men, and then ten men, and then the whole team, but each time Fionn succeeded. While the team played with great intensity, the skill of Fionn could not be matched.

At the end of the evening's long training, Iollan knew his team finally had a chance of winning the black bull of Aughnacloy — he was staring right at him. 'What's your name?'

'Fionn.'

Looking at his exhausted players, Iollan continued, 'Will you play for us?'

'I will, on one condition.'

'What is it?'

'In every team I have played on I have always been captain.'

Iollan had been captain for the last two years and he knew this year would be his last before he became too old. But he also knew that his injured knee meant he would not play again this summer, and his team needed a leader. With the eyes of Cana and his teammates on him, Iollan agreed that Fionn would be made the first ever freelance captain of the hurlers of Donard.

• • •

Over the few days, Fionn got to know more about his new team. This meant that when everyone came together in Cana and Iollan's home on the morning of the game, he knew exactly who he was going to select and where they were going to play. The team was similar to the one Iollan had assembled the week before, until he announced the last person to be selected.

'For number fifteen, starting in the corner upfront, I am selecting Cana.'

The place erupted in yells of disagreement about the surprise inclusion.

'A girl!' cried Fergal.

'No way,' shouted Martan.

'Never!' Senán called out.

'I won't play,' yelled Barra.

'I'm hungry,' exclaimed Riordan, the goalkeeper, who had missed his lunch.

'Fine,' Fionn finally roared, bringing quiet to the room. 'Don't play if you don't want to. However, I am captain. Iollan made it so. And you know as well as I do that the captain always chooses the team. And I choose Cana. If you don't want to play and there are only fourteen players — or even just the two of us — then so be it. But that is my team and I am the captain.'

To his left, Iollan, whose face had grown as red as his hair, looked at Fionn with fire in his eyes before storming out. However, to his right, Cana was smiling and gripping her hurl very tightly.

That afternoon, Clan Rooney fared much better, seeing off Clan Mahon by several points. While the team were much improved by having Fionn to the fore, they could have won by more if the players had chosen to pass to Cana when she was free or looked to collect a pass off her when she did have the sliotar. But their anger had seeped into the game, so that throughout the match she was widely ignored. Fionn knew this had to change. They were six matches from the final and the competition would only get tougher. Everybody needed to stick together; otherwise they would be torn apart. As they returned home, it was tradition for them to stop at the Kilcoo springs to allow their tired bodies soak and recover. It was here that Fionn challenged his players.

'We played well today, but we could have played better. You chose to not be a team and to play for yourselves rather than for each other. If you really don't want Cana to play with you, then you will need to take the captaincy. And I am willing to give it up to any one of you who can outscore Cana by striking sliotars over the bar. But if you can't outscore her this ends here and we start playing like a team.'

It was a risk, but Fionn trusted in Cana's skill. He wasn't disappointed. The team lined up against her. Even her brother Iollan with his gammy knee, who was still angry that Fionn had tricked him into allowing his sister on to the team. But to their surprise she outscored them all.

And in the next game, the risk paid off. In their toughest match to date against the Clan Lionnáin of Crossmaglen, whom they had lost to last year, they gave everything they got and more. Fionn ran the show in midfield and Cana scored with ease up front, and by the end they were convincing victors.

As the weeks progressed, the team went from strength to strength. They steadily beat one team after the next until they had just one match to win in order to progress to the great Ulster final on the legendary hurling fields of Emain Macha. Just as they had expected, it was to be against their nemesis, Clan Lochlainn, who lived south of the body of water known as Cúan Cairlinne.

One night after training, Fionn asked the team about Clan Lochlainn. 'Who are these people and why do you hate them so much?'

'At one time we were close to Clan Lochlainn,' Cana explained, 'but then a split occurred in the Fianna between Clan Morna and Clan Bascna. The Lochlainns had supported the Mornas. Meanwhile, many from Clan Rooney swore fealty to Clan Bascna under Cumhall. What had once been a friendly rivalry turned to bitter enmity after Cumhall was banished. Our men didn't leave with Clan Bascna when they left the High King's service to travel westwards in search of Cumhall. They stayed at Tara first but then returned home to Donard when word came of Cumhall's death at the Battle of Cnucha. Since then we haven't sent any of our sons into the Fianna's service. In response, cattle raids have occurred along our southern border and our men have been attacked, but the High King has provided no justice.'

After hearing that Clan Rooney were once loyal to his own family, a part of Fionn longed to share with Cana who he really was – but he held back. Not yet. 'I'm guessing this match against them won't be a quiet one then,' Fionn said with a smile.

'Probably not,' Cana answered.

• • •

A week later, they faced Clan Lochlainn on the fields of Annaclone. Clan Donard knew what lay ahead of them. From the look of at least two of their forward line, they knew that Clan Lochlainn had a couple of older inclusions in their team, most likely Fianna warriors.

What Clan Rooney and Fionn did not realise was that word had finally travelled about a young boy with bright blond hair setting the Ulster hurling championship alight with his displays of brilliance. These rumours had reached Goll and most of his men, who had been fighting down south against the rebel forces of three Kerry kings. Goll feared that only the young son of his great rival could possess such skill and decided it was time to act. He brought his battles with the Kerry kings to an abrupt end and gathered his troops for a quick march northward. As they set off, he sent word ahead to the Lochlainns that if they had the chance to deal with this boy, on or off the field, they should take it.

• • •

The semi-final was not a pretty spectacle, with Clan Lochlainn more interested in playing the body, not the ball, and Fionn's body in particular. However, despite all their attempts, Fionn could not be caught. He defended himself against every chop, every belt and every wild swing. The game was tight. It hinged on one key moment when Cana, with hair tucked behind her ear, cut the ball off the ground and sent it tall, sharp and clean over the bar! Then came a succession of scores by Clan Rooney from which the Lochlainns never recovered. There were cuts, bruises and bumps, but the hurlers of Donard prevailed. An Ulster final now beckoned.

Although Fionn had escaped injury on the field, Clan Lochlainn had a back-up plan. As his teammates left the field, Fionn was called back to be congratulated by the chief of their arch-rivals. He was held back for a long time as they complimented him on how he had played. By the time Fionn got to the Kilcoo springs, his teammates were about to leave.

'Go on without me,' Fionn told them as he entered the healing water. 'I'll see you later.'

As Fionn's teammates left for Donard, the players of Clan Lochlainn crept from where they had been hiding. The chief's long praise-filled speech had been a trap and Fionn was now exactly where they wanted him.

CRASH! Fionn, who had been floating in the shallows, opened his eyes to see the Lochlainns descending on him, waving hurls and throwing fists. Jumping to his feet, he immediately began defending himself with equal vigour. But he was outnumbered almost twenty to one and soon the blows and punches were weakening him. Fionn retreated to the deeper water, but the Lochlainns followed, trying to pull him down and drown him. However, Fionn was as strong a swimmer as his mother Muirne had been. He held his own, at least for a while.

After a half-hour, however, the heat of the fight abated as the initial strength of the Lochlainns left them. But so too was the adrenaline of battle now wearing off for Fionn. As each member of Clan Lochlainn took a turn tackling him, Fionn sank deeper. It soon seemed unlikely that he would see the next day, let alone the final.

But just as Fionn was losing hope, a roar began to grow from deep in the woods. Suddenly, with as much gusto as they had during the game, Cana and the whole team ploughed into their rivals, who had encircled a struggling Fionn. The game was a close affair, but the fight afterwards wasn't. Armed with their hurls, Clan Donard trounced Clan Lochlainn and sent them packing.

'Quick,' shouted Iollan, pointing to Fionn. 'Help him out.' The team lifted Fionn's near-lifeless body from the spring and carried him home to Donard.

• • •

'Morning.'

Fionn's vision was a little fuzzy but he could recognise Cana's voice. 'Morning,' he replied hoarsely. 'What happened?'

'We beat Clan Lochlainn. Then they beat you. And then we beat them again.'

'How did you know to come back for me?'

'I didn't,' Cana answered. 'It was Iollan's idea. He didn't think it was right that we arrived home without our captain on our shoulders. It isn't every day that we beat Clan Lochlainn. As it turns out, however, we brought you home not on our shoulders but on a stretcher.'

Fionn smiled, sensing the humour in Cana's voice.

'There's more,' she continued. 'Your secret is out, Fionn, or should I say Fionn Mac Cumhaill?'

'How did you find out?'

'Well, I can't speak for the rest of the boys, but I think I always knew,' Cana said. 'A freelance shepherd armed to the teeth when a wolf hasn't been seen on the Mournes in a generation. And then there was your skill in learning how to hurl. I am not that good a teacher! As for outside the clan, it seems that word had got out about a young boy with exceptional skill who was running rings around every team in Ulster. Word has also reached Goll Mac Morna, who is travelling up from Munster as we speak. Clan Lochlainn were to either kill you or hurt you enough that there would be little left for the Mac Mornas to deal with.'

'They did a pretty good job,' Fionn croaked.

'They did, but not good enough.'

'What day is it?' Fionn enquired.

'It's two days since the fight and a day before you leave us.'

'What of the final next weekend?'

'We'll have to fight that final ourselves,' Cana said. 'You're not safe here anymore. At the final Goll and his men will be at the side of the field wondering exactly who this young man is and sharpening their weapons for when you come off it. Besides, I'm guessing that you can barely walk, let alone run.'

Fionn was crestfallen. Sensing his sadness, Cana put his hand in hers. 'Fionn, the lads will always be grateful to you for bringing them this far, and I will always be grateful to you for helping me to play the game I love and for representing my people. You will always be able to count on us as friends and one day we will serve under you as captain once again. But you need to leave for your own safety.'

Cana was right. As much as it pained him to leave Clan Rooney and the young hurlers of Donard, it was time to go.

'How can I travel in this state?' he asked.

'We have someone who will be as slow as you, Fionn. But he will help you get there,' said Cana. And with that, Iollan limped into the room. 'Iollan knows these mountains, hills, valleys and glens better than anyone. As Goll and his men march north on Emain Macha, you'll march south past them.'

'But what of the team? Now that I am gone, who will lead you out in the final?'

'Don't worry, I know just the person,' Iollan answered, smiling at his sister.

• • •

A few weeks later, Fionn landed at Loch Luimnigh, which would later become known as Limerick. He had bid Iollan goodbye near Lough Erne before criss-crossing over to the great Shannon river, down which he sailed. When he came ashore for some food and water, he overheard a conversation take place between two old men about the greatest game that Emain Macha had seen in generations.

It had been a true clash of the ash — a match between two mighty teams that had been settled with the final puck of the game. As the sun set behind the Armagh hills, the female captain of Clan Donard, a girl by the name of Cana, had jumped high into the air to grab hold of the sliotar. She had then struck it clear, far and straight over the bar.

To Fionn's delight, one of the old men said that the whole Fianna force were there and that their leader, Goll, had been asked to present the prize to the captain of Clan Rooney — something that seemed to give Goll immense displeasure for some reason. The tale warmed Fionn's heart as he prepared to embark on his next adventure in the kingdoms of Kerry.

THE KINGDOMS OF KERRY

If Fionn thought that by coming to the Celtic kingdoms of Kerry he could forget about Goll Mac Morna, he was mistaken. Yes, Goll had wrongly guessed that Fionn would play in the Ulster hurling final. And he had foolishly brought his forces all the way to Emain Macha to capture and kill Fionn — only to discover that Fionn had escaped his grasp once more. But until a few weeks ago, Goll had been fighting in this part of the land for more than two seasons. The devastating effects of him and his Fianna warriors were everywhere, from the burnt-out huts to the families still mourning their dead. His name and that of the Fianna were now spoken of with hatred.

Kerry had long been a part of an Ireland that saw itself as a separate kingdom. Indeed, it was only recently that the three kings who ruled the three kingdoms of Kerry had allowed their realms to be overseen by a High King of Ireland. They had agreed on the conditions that the Fianna would always abide by three ancient mottoes — 'purity in our hearts, strength in our limbs and truth on our lips' — and that the High King would rule in the best interests of all Ireland and not just for his family and friends. But since the split in the Fianna and then the death of Cumhall, this had not been the case. Under Goll Mac Morna, the Fianna were no longer an honourable force but a violent band of thieves and brigands that grew more corrupt with each passing winter. Meanwhile, although the High King had got rid of the corrosive influence of Tadg, his Chief Druid, he was getting older and no longer had the strength, wisdom or power of a true High King. All of these changes had caused the King of Listowel, the King of Iveragh and the King of Aghadoe to break away from his oversight. It had been this desire for independence that Goll and his men were seeking to crush when news of Fionn playing in the Ulster final drew them northwards.

• • •

The first kingdom Fionn entered was the stronghold of Listowel. It stretched from the village of Tarbert to the Blasket Islands off the Dingle Peninsula. When his strength had fully returned after his injuries at the hands of Clan Lochlainn, Fionn joined a band of hunters in the service of the local king, Anlon. He told no one who he was. However, word soon reached King Anlon of a newcomer who had no equal as a hunter. Anlon wanted to meet this young man and thank him for providing many of his people with food, which was badly needed as the Kingdom of Listowel had been greatly damaged by Goll's attacks.

King Anlon had once feasted at Tara with Cumhall and the Fianna, and he immediately recognised someone in Fionn. However, he couldn't quite put his finger on who it was he saw in him.

'What is your name, my boy?' Anlon asked as he sat down beside Fionn at the feasting table.

'Daire,' Fionn lied.

'And who was your father?'

'His name was Daig, a small herdsman from the south-east, but he is dead now.'

'I'm sorry to hear that.'

As the feast progressed, the king continued studying the young lad. There was something in the way the young boy ate that made a long-forgotten memory bubble up in him.

'Cumhall!'

'Excuse me, my lord?' said Fionn.

'Cumhall. That's who you remind me of. Although you are too young to have known him, you are the image of Cumhall of Clan Bascna, the former proud leader of the Fianna.'

At the mere mention of the Fianna, the hunters sitting nearby grew uneasy and began to glance at Fionn with suspicion. Not knowing whether the king held his father in high esteem or regarded him with loathing, Fionn became nervous in case Anlon had not believed his story. So, that night, as his fellow hunters slept, Fionn packed up his few belongings and set off further south.

• • •

Fionn spent the next couple of days travelling south until he reached the next realm of Kerry: the great peninsula Kingdom of Iveragh. The Kingdom of Iveragh was dominated by a vast mountain range called Na Cruacha Dubha. It ran from Dún Lóich in the east to the towering summit of Carrauntoohil, before fanning out westwards and finally ending at the wild islands of Na Sceallaga. Although Fionn could have hidden here for a very long time, only having to worry about the great packs of wolves that roamed the hilly woodlands, he was unable to continue leading a solitary life, so he became a soldier for the King of Iveragh, King Cearbhall. Once again, Fionn's talent stood out. One day, when Cearbhall was visiting the camp, he noticed Fionn's skill at brandubh and challenged him to a contest. Having been taught the game by his foster mother Breac — a master at this game — Fionn's skill was remarkable. He prevailed not once, not twice, but seven times. He even began copying Breac's habit of suggesting the moves his competitor should play! Cearbhall was outraged.

'Who are you?' he demanded.

'My name is Fiachu. I'm the son of a poor farmer from the east,' answered Fionn.

'You are not,' the king replied with fury. 'I now recognise your face. You are the son of Cumhall, former leader of the Fianna and nemesis of Goll Mac Morna. Leave here at once. I cannot protect you. If Goll hears of your presence here, we will not escape the devastation that has befallen the Kingdom of Listowel at the hands of him and his men.'

Fionn knew that it was once again time to leave.

• • •

He travelled east and soon reached the final kingdom of Kerry — the Kingdom of Aghadoe. Word of his identity was beginning to spread, so he felt that he need not keep his name a secret. When he entered the court of the king, he announced, 'My name is Fionn Mac Cumhaill, son of Cumhall — the last great leader of the Fianna. I am trying to stay ahead of the clutches of Goll Mac Morna and his men. I ask that you grant me some food and a place to rest tonight.'

Fionn expected to receive the response of a ruler who wished him gone. But to his joyful surprise, King Rian declared that not only was his family loyal to Clan Bascna, but he would also shelter and protect Fionn for as long as he could. True to his word, over the next month Fionn received a year's worth of hospitality. He ate at court and enjoyed his time in the company of this family friend, who quickly became like an uncle to him. As the weeks passed, however, he could feel despair hanging like a shadow over the kingdom. At first, he thought it was the aftermath of Goll's campaign of violence, which had devastated the poorest of Kerry's three kingdoms. But soon he realised it was something much more than that and he became determined to find out what was wrong. At supper one evening, he saw a chance.

'King Rian, there is something that has been bothering me,' Fionn began. 'I feel that there is a darkness that hangs over your land. When I swim or fish in Lough Leane, villagers warn me not to stray too close to its southern shore. At night, they lock their windows and doors as if the evil Dealra Dubh were coming to visit them. I sense that, whatever it is, people believe it begins on the mountain overlooking the lake and then pours forth into the great forested area that surrounds its base.'

Putting down the leg of meat he had been chewing on, Rian looked sombrely at Fionn. 'They do not fear the mountain but what lives on it. A magical wild boar has roamed there for many moons now. This evil and malevolent beast is thought to have come from the Otherworld by passing through a sidhe mound that connects both realms.'

Fionn had overheard Bodhmall and Breac talking about the Otherworld. It was a parallel universe where a supernatural race was said to exist, which could only be accessed through sidhe or fairy mounds. He had been young then, and when he asked about it — frightened of the beasts that were said to live on the other side — they told him not to worry. They said that these sidhe mounds had long since been sealed and that there were very few spirits on the island now.

'I thought the sidhe mounds had all been sealed?' Fionn said.

'They were,' Rian replied, 'but over the last few years they have been broken open. Some say it has been thieves, looking to get the treasure that was hidden underneath as payment for good spirits standing guard and staving off creatures that might try to break through to our world. No one really knows. These sidhes were once protected by the Fianna, who would reward a trespasser who broke the seal with death. Now the Fianna serve justice to no one and are said to receive a share from these raids. It was from one of these sidhes in the south of our kingdom that this evil wild boar was released. Since then, it has terrorised the surrounding villages and taken the life of anyone who had the misfortune of coming too close to the mountain.'

'Surely someone has tried to kill it?' Fionn wondered.

'We have tried. Some of our best warriors left the battles with Goll to journey into the woods to defeat it. But none have succeeded — and many have failed to return. Those who did come back spoke of a wild boar with intelligence and cunning unseen in any other animal. A beast with tusks that tear and slash, with a skin that is almost impenetrable to their weapons.'

Following a moment of silence, Fionn spoke. 'I will hunt down and kill this beast. You have welcomed me as if I were your own family in spite of the risk to your people. And I will return that kindness by ridding you of this fiend. All I ask is that one day you be loyal to me, in the same way you were loyal to my father.'

Fionn had not seen fifteen winters. Although he was athletic, he lacked the build and the muscle of King Rian's strongest warriors. But despite this, Rian could see in Fionn something that set him apart from others — a belief in himself, an air of quiet confidence and a sense of someone who would make history.

'By my honour, I will,' the king replied.

The next morning, before the sun had risen, Fionn was on his way to the clan's blacksmith, a man by the name of Lochan. Fionn hoped the blacksmith would arm him for what lay ahead.

• • •

'... but when he got home, he made a bolt for the door!'

Lochan could hear the voice of a stranger inside, followed by the unmistakable laugh of his daughter.

'You're laughing, but I still don't get it,' the stranger continued.

'A bolt. Like a bolt you would close a door with, not "to bolt", like run away,' his daughter answered, still chuckling.

'Oh ... I get it now.'

'Get what now?' Lochan interrupted. At over six feet tall, he had to stoop to enter through the front door.

'A joke, Dad, a joke,' replied his fiery-haired daughter, Cnes. 'Dad, this is Fionn. He came here early this morning looking for you. I invited him in so he wouldn't have to spend the day outside with the hens. It was a good decision — he's been sharing his cooking skills with me all morning.'

'And what have you been doing?' Lochan asked his daughter. He continued viewing the newcomer with suspicion.

'Putting my feet up with a well-earned reward for inviting him in,' Cnes replied, gesturing to her bowl of stew.

'What is your business?' Lochan asked Fionn.

'King Rian suggested that I ask you to arm me.'

'Why?'

'I am going to kill the wild boar that terrorises this land.'

'You never said that!' Cnes interrupted, a trace of anger in her voice.

'You never asked,' replied Fionn.

Cnes got up and walked straight out of the house, slamming the door on her way out.

'What did I say?' Fionn asked, surprised at Cnes's reaction.

'Her mother — my wife — was killed several moons ago by that beast,' Lochan answered. His eyes were still on the door, which had nearly been knocked off its hinges by his daughter's exit.

'I'm sorry,' said Fionn.

'Don't be. It's not your fault,' Lochan said. 'Few have come close to defeating it, so my daughter is upset that someone she has just befriended will now meet a nasty end.'

'Befriended?'

'You've been here since morning and you don't have two black eyes. That's a friend in Cnes's book anyway. It's the first time I've heard her laugh in quite some time.'

'Well, she needn't worry,' Fionn confidently replied. 'I don't intend to die.'

'And neither did any of the other two dozen warriors who came through here looking to be armed, but Torc had other ideas.'

'Torc?'

'Yes, Torc. That's what we call the beast,' Lochan answered. 'Anyway, if it's well-armed you want to be, then I have the weapon for you.' Lochan went into his workshop, where a noisy racket could soon be heard. A short time later he re-emerged. 'Found it. I knew I had hidden it somewhere safe.' In Lochan's hands was a finely forged spear that showed all the signs of a true craftsman.

• • •

That evening, Fionn and Lochan ate together. But there was an empty chair where Cnes usually sat.

'Is she all right?' Fionn asked.

'She's fine. She's probably gone to the court of King Rian. Since her mother died, she has begun working there some days. It's good for her to get out and be somewhere safe,' Lochan replied. 'She is wonderful — bright and funny but also as stubborn as her mother was.'

'Did she have fiery red hair as well?' Fionn asked.

Lochan smiled. 'She did. Cnes misses her terribly, as I do. Hearing that you were going to hunt the beast upset her, that's all.'

'What happened?' Fionn asked without thinking. He collected himself. 'Sorry, I didn't ...'

'It's fine,' said Lochan. 'My wife, Neacht, was like everyone around here. She was careful not to get too close to the forest for fear of the beast. But one morning she woke to find Cnes gone and the sound of screams coming from the woods. A neighbour saw Neacht running towards the cries. He told my wife that it was too dangerous to enter on her own and that he would return with the king's warriors. But Neacht could not bear to think of Cnes all alone in the forest — so she went to find her.'

'What happened?'

'I met that neighbour, along with King Rian and his men, when I returned from work with Cnes beside me.'

'Huh?'

'Cnes often came with me on my journeys. Early that morning, she sneaked away with me without her mother's knowledge.'

'So, if it wasn't Cnes, whose cries were they?'

'Probably that of a púca, a wicked shape-shifting spirit common in these parts. It likes to trick us innocent mortals and lead us astray. We'll never know. Those screams were never heard again, nor those of my love. All that could be found of her when we entered the woods was her hair bow and the large bloodstained hoofprints of what could only have been Torc. I wanted to go further, and it took every ounce of strength of the king and his warriors to pull me back out of the woods. The king demanded that I not make Cnes an orphan.'

Silence fell between them. With nothing more to say, they returned to their food.

• • •

By the clear cloven hoofprints he had been carefully following for the last few hours, Fionn was sure that he was on the trail of a wild boar. And by the monstrous size of them he was certain that it was the trail of the beast they called Torc. But the lair to which the trail had led was so clean — too clean and tidy to be that of a horrible wild beast. Admittedly, he hadn't seen many boar dens, so he didn't know what they looked like, but he could not imagine them to be so neat. As well as that, boars usually lived in thick brush to protect them from predators, but this lair was out in the open. Whoever lived here had few predators.

'You're wondering whether you've found his lair, aren't you?'

Fionn swung round, spear in hand. At first, he could not see the owner of the voice. Then there was a rustling in the deep, dark undergrowth and the figure of Cnes emerged.

'You never wished me well this morning,' he said, trying to contain both his surprise and irritation at being caught unawares.

'Sorry about that, but I thought you wouldn't want me tagging along with you. I guessed you'd soon pick up Torc's trail and that I'd find you at his lair. So, I came here to wait for you.' With that, she threw Fionn a small satchel.

'What's this?' he asked.

'Open it and find out.'

When Fionn unbuttoned the bag, he was hit with an overwhelming, earthy stench that made his knees wobble. 'Urgh!'

Cnes laughed. 'Kerry's finest purple stinkhorn mushrooms. Perfume of the forest floor, I like to call them.'

'What are they for?'

'They're like perfume, only different. You put some on so you don't get noticed,' she replied, smiling. She began to rub some of the mushrooms onto her face, hair and clothes. 'I strongly advise you to do the same. It'll be here soon.'

'What will?'

'Torc. Now, quickly, rub this on yourself and follow me.'

Fionn swiftly smeared his face, hair and clothes with the putrid-smelling mushrooms before withdrawing into the undergrowth after Cnes. When they were some distance away but still had sight of the lair, they hunkered down and waited.

'How do you know it is the beast's lair?' Fionn whispered.

'First, because I've seen Torc here several times before. Second, because I learned that wild boars, even supernatural ones, are not as dirty as we humans think. They're actually quite clean and, no matter how monstrous they are, they keep their lairs spotless. Except, of course, for their mud bath.'

'Mud bath?'

'Yes, a mud bath. Don't you know that everyone in Kerry has a mud bath?'

For a moment, Fionn almost believed her.

'Boars like mud baths. In fact, more than like them, they need them. Torc's bath is there in the corner,' Cnes said, motioning over his shoulder to the lair.

Fionn was gobsmacked. He had already been shocked that Cnes had been waiting for him in this most dangerous of forests. And now she was telling him things about a beast that had killed countless warriors before him. It took him a moment to take it all in. A raft of questions came to his mind. 'You were here before? Why didn't you tell me this? And what makes you so special that you can survive when so many have been killed?'

'That's a lot of questions,' Cnes replied. 'But let me answer the easier ones first. I didn't tell you because my dad doesn't know I come here. He thinks that when I leave the house, I go to the court of Aghadoe in the service of King Rian.'

'And do you?'

'Yes, sometimes, but not as often as my father thinks. Next, I'm not special. I've just learned quickly. When my mother died, I knew that I would have my revenge. But I also knew that many warriors had already failed in their attempts to kill the beast. I decided that if I could not kill him with brawn, for these warriors were much stronger and more skilful than I, I would kill him with brains. I travelled to Rian's royal court and sought out his oldest and wisest druid, who told me everything you could ever know about wild boars. The druid's name was Phelim. He liked to answer my questions with riddles and rhymes, so it took time to understand what he was saying, but eventually I learned enough to know that I was ready to confront the beast.'

'What sort of rhymes?' Fionn asked.

'I am evil and mean, but always stay clean. What am I?'

'A pig or a boar?' Fionn guessed, and Cnes nodded. 'But I don't understand,' he said.

'Everyone knows this beast is mean,' Cnes said, 'and everyone also thinks that a wild boar is dirty and messy, but it's not. It keeps its den clean.'

'And that's how you knew this lair was Torc's?'

'Well, that's how I guessed this lair was Torc's. I knew it was when I saw Torc here.'

'How did it not notice you?'

'As Phelim said, "Sight, sound, touch and taste, one of these is such a waste. As for the one that is missing, this is why I know you're visiting."'

'That doesn't rhyme very well,' Fionn said with a grin.

'I said that the druid was a wise man. I never said he was a great poet. Anyway, I figured that, considering that those who crossed it ended up as its evening meal, its senses of touch and taste must be fine. As for the other two, I always got the impression from the boars that were reared in the village that they heard me sneaking up on them long before they saw me. As time went on, I realised that they weren't great at seeing at all. But I guessed from the riddle that their greatest sense must be their ability to smell. So, to protect myself from the beast I played around with the strongest-smelling woodland odours that I could find in order to smother my scent.'

'The stinkhorn mushrooms.'

'Yes, the stinkhorns. After that, I started entering the woods. I moved slowly and didn't go far at first. But as dangerous as it was, I was determined to find this monster.'

'What were you hoping to do?' Fionn asked.

'Kill it, of course. But the day I first saw it, I knew.'

'Knew what?'

Almost on cue, Cnes grabbed Fionn's arm and put her finger to her lips. 'Shhh. It's here.'

A wild boar came into view on the other side of the lair. It must have been three times the size of the biggest boar Fionn had ever hunted, and its tusks were as long and sharp as swords.

Cnes breathed softly. 'I knew that I would never be able to get near it. And even if I were to, well, look closely at its body,' she whispered.

Fionn gazed intensely at the beast until he saw what Cnes had seen. The beast was covered not just with hair but with ... scales? 'A wild boar with scales? What sort of evil is that?'

'I know. That is one more reason why no warrior has ever killed it. Torc's scales are its armour. But that's not all. "Feel brave, step near. Kneel down, raw ear."'

'Another rhyme. What does it mean?'

'It is the last reason why the beast is almost invincible. Torc has a squeal so highly pitched it can bring down a horse and make the most resolute of men powerless. It makes it impossible to get near Torc.'

'Has anyone ever come close to killing it, then?'

'Just once, by a brave warrior named Uallgarg. Uallgarg was famed for his throwing ability and had a celebrated spear that seemed to sing when he cast it. But Uallgarg never heard it sing, because he was deaf. After my mother was killed, he led a group of warriors chosen by the king to track and kill the beast. They managed to corner Torc, but, although his fellow warriors had their ears blocked with wet moss, the squeals were so great that they were soon driven back. Not Uallgarg, however. Instead, he stepped forward, took aim and fired. His spear caught the boar with such force that it had no right to remain alive. But it survived and fled, squealing in pain. Picking up his spear, he found a great scale attached. And if you look under its front right hock, you can see it hasn't grown back. That's where it's vulnerable – that's how you will kill it.'

Fionn looked closely at this point of weakness. He asked, 'Why didn't Uallgarg return to finish it off?'

'The boar didn't let him,' Cnes replied. 'He and his men returned home and prepared to hunt again the next morning, but the beast ambushed them in the night. He killed Uallgarg first before attacking the others. By the time the men rallied, Uallgarg was mortally wounded and more than half of the others were dead or injured. No one has come close since.'

As she spoke, Fionn could see Torc slowly making its way towards the mud bath. He made to rise but Cnes grabbed his arm. 'Not yet. Not now. There's more you need to know first.' And with that, Cnes and Fionn tiptoed away from his lair.

• • •

That evening, over food in their makeshift camp, Fionn enquired, 'What's our plan? Return tomorrow, plug our ears with moss, wait for it and kill it?'

'Not quite,' Cnes answered. 'The beast is intelligent. It knows it is vulnerable and won't make the mistake of exposing itself. And that's where the old druid's final riddle comes in — "I quickly rise in great fury, in anger and in sound, but it takes me a lot longer to eventually cool down."'

'I don't understand?'

'The beast, like all wild boars, can't cool down like we can. It doesn't sweat — that's why it has its mud bath.'

'So what? We're going to drain the mud bath?'

'No,' Cnes chuckled. 'We are going to make it sweat so much that it will overheat, become confused and make mistakes. That's when it will drop its guard, and that's when you strike.'

'And how will we make him sweat?'

'Did you ever play tag as a child?' Cnes asked with a grin.

• • •

The next morning, Fionn sat patiently as Cnes went through the route they would travel and explained to him that Torc took the same path at the same time each day. As a result, they were now waiting on the eastern face of the mountain. From her weeks of observation, she expected Torc to pass through around noon, the warmest part of the day.

The plan was that when Torc got close, Cnes would make noise enough to have it give chase. Once that happened the hunt would begin. Cnes would run as hard as she could to keep far enough ahead of Torc to be almost out of sight. It was over two miles around the mountain and when she came within sight of Fionn she would then dive off the path into a deep thicket of bush to catch her breath ahead for one final loop while Fionn began his turn. Fionn had asked to go first but Cnes had convinced him otherwise. Her job was to tire Torc out, Fionn's was to take advantage of this.

'Are you sure?' he asked her. Although Fionn might not have liked to admit it, he was glad to have the company of a friend in what would surely be a dangerous game of cat and mouse. But he also feared this new-found friend would come to harm.

'As sure as someone who is going to be chased by a wild evil boar that killed her mother,' Cnes answered darkly. 'Don't worry, I've been waiting many moons for this moment. I'll be fine. Just make sure you don't miss.'

Not long after, they caught a glimpse of Torc through the trees. And it was cantering towards them! 'Right, here I go,' Cnes said, putting the damp moss she had moulded into her ears. With a nod to Fionn, she mouthed 'Good luck' and took off shouting. A few moments later, the beast charged by, hot on her heels. It was emitting a squeal that, even with earplugs, brought Fionn to his knees. As the boar disappeared, he stepped out from his hiding place, took his position and waited.

Not a quarter of an hour later, he could hear distant squeals. They were coming closer, which meant that the boar was still charging — which meant that Cnes was still running!

A minute later, Cnes came dashing down the track. Seeing Fionn, she braved a smile before diving for cover. As she did, the boar hurtled around the bend. If it was tired, it didn't look it — not yet anyway. Fionn let out a battle cry and set off running. He repeated the circuit, keeping ahead of the beast. Just as his legs were starting to tire, he reached the end of his circuit and dived into the undergrowth as Cnes took off once more.

Cnes's second — and final — lap was the toughest. Fionn didn't know how much time had passed but it felt so much longer than the first. The squeals had also stopped. Fionn could not help but worry. Had Torc caught her? Had it killed her? Why the delay? Time seemed to slow down. But as his mind began to fill with a feeling of dread, he saw her — cheeks red, sweat dripping, head dropping. She staggered the last few steps and collapsed onto the ground beside him.

Fionn strode towards Torc, who had just come into sight — heaving for breath, legs wobbling, disorientated and no longer squealing. Fionn could see that its scales held not a bead of sweat. And then he saw the exposed area that Uallgarg's spear had uncovered. With a hunter's instinct, he pulled back his arm to launch his spear — but then hesitated. Torc was drained of energy, but Fionn knew if he did not make his mark, the beast still had enough strength to kill them both. Instead, Fionn charged at the beast and thrust the full force of his spear through Torc's exposed flesh, killing the fiend. The Kingdom of Aghadoe was finally rid of this wild malevolent, beastly boar. The site of this victory by Fionn and Cnes would from that day forward be known as Torc Mountain.

• • •

Fionn and Cnes came down from the mountain and into the arms of Lochan and King Rian. As both were greeted with love, relief and affection, a great cheer went up from the locals. But the joy at the news of the beast's death did not last for long. Rian had been informed that Goll now knew of Fionn's presence in the kingdom. A large band of the Fianna were travelling south with instructions to capture or kill him.

'Fionn,' said Rian, 'I am eternally grateful for what you did for us, and one day I will repay that debt in full. But you will need to leave for Connacht now, before Goll arrives.'

'Why Connacht?' Fionn asked.

'Your father's brother, Crimmal, is in a remote forest in the bogs of deepest Connemara, waiting with the last remnants of his and your father's clan and those who remained loyal to Cumhall.'

'Waiting for what?'

'For you, Fionn. For you.'

THE GREY OF LUACHRA

A week after he wished Cnes, her father Lochan and King Rian farewell, Fionn found himself sitting on what felt like the very edge of the world itself. As he sat high on the great rocky cliff that looked out to the open ocean, he wondered if he would ever get used to saying goodbye to people he had grown to love. Despite making more friends in the last few months than he had in his whole life, he had never felt more alone. He would have spent the rest of his journey northwards in search of his uncle Crimmal in this state of misery had he not come across someone whose sadness would overshadow his own.

It was an early morning, when the seasons were beginning to change and a crisp fog hung closely to the ground, that he came across the widow Marga. He was in a part of the west that would become known as Clare. At first, he had thought it was a cat that was wailing, but as he approached, he became worried that it was the keening of a banshee, whose piercing song was predicting the death of a loved one. But when Fionn arrived at its source – an old hut with a thin trail of smoke rising from its chimney – he discovered that the cries came from an old woman. Death had already visited here. An elderly woman was wailing and swaying with grief, smeared with blood from the body of the young man who lay in her arms.

'What's happened?' Fionn asked her. 'Who is this man?'

At first the old woman failed to respond, but after some time the strength left her cries, and in a grave whisper she answered Fionn. 'This is my only son, Lonán, who has been taken from me. Last night, we welcomed a stranger into our home and gave him food and drink, as is our custom. I awoke to the sound of a cry. When I lit a rush candle, I discovered my son had been murdered – stabbed through the back – and the stranger gone. Gone with him were three silver goblets that we received from the High King of Ireland many years ago in thanks for the service of my husband, who died protecting this island from Scottish invaders. This stranger, this thief, this murderer, has taken them — along with the life of my only son.'

'What did this stranger look like?'

'He was tall and thin with hair as grey as clouds of thunder. He smiled when he spoke, a smile that hid a wicked heart.' She began to wail once more.

Fionn stayed a while, not wanting to leave the woman in such a grievous state. Soon, four young riders approached, two boys and two girls not much older than Fionn. One of the boys spoke. 'We are from Clan Halpin, the clan that this household belongs to. What has happened here that has left our young cousin dead and Marga — his mother and our aunt — in such distress?'

Fionn recounted to them the story he had just been told. 'I will track this thief down and avenge this poor woman's loss,' he announced.

The cousins thanked Fionn for his service. The eldest cousin, a boy named Fearghal, declared that he and his siblings Keelan and Niamh would join Fionn in his pursuit, while the youngest would stay behind to look after the widow. Although none of them were warriors, they could not leave a stranger to search alone for a villain who had killed one of their own.

• • •

Steadily following Fearghal, Fionn pulled out a finely wrought brooch from inside his cloak and traced its pattern with his finger. The pain in Marga's eyes had made him think of his own mother. He wondered if she had felt the same pain when she had said goodbye to him when he was just a newborn. In the fourteen years since, his mother Muirne had been able to visit him only once, briefly, when he was six. Late one night, when he was half-asleep, she had visited him at the hut of Bodhmall and Breac. The memory was half-real, half-dream, but she had left a silver brooch. That was his proof it had happened. She never visited again — not out of fear for her safety, but for Fionn's, in case Goll or his men were to follow her. Fionn wondered if he would ever see her again or if, like Marga, he would have to wait until the next world to be reunited with his family.

• • •

For the whole day, Fionn and the three cousins travelled in pursuit of the tall, thin man. Despite the late-September rain, Fionn had been able to find the trail of a solitary traveller. He pursued it closely until Keelan took over that evening. When darkness fell and most people retreated to the warmth of their shelters, they persevered.

That doggedness finally brought them to the sight of a campfire on a barren, rocky landscape.

'There, in the distance, flickering in the mist.' Keelan from Clan Halpin was directing Fionn's attention to a small blaze up ahead.

'That is no hut or home,' responded Niamh. 'Few people live on this stony land, and no one lives where that fire burns.'

'I ask that you let me go alone from here,' Fionn said. 'If this is the man your aunt has spoken of, he will not be taken without a fight. And that is something I am ready for.'

'If this is the man my aunt has spoken about,' Niamh said, 'then he is as smart as he is evil. Don't turn your back on him.'

As Fionn came closer to the fire, he could see the silhouette of a man against the blaze. The figure was sitting behind the fallen bough of an old tree, which now served as his table.

'Hello,' Fionn called out. 'May I join you and the warmth of your fire?'

On hearing this, the man rose. Fionn could see that he was tall and slim. The flames illuminated his unmistakable mane of grey hair.

When the stranger saw Fionn's youthful appearance, he relaxed and sat back down. 'Yes, come sit down here with me. I have only begun my supper. You are welcome to share what little I have.'

In front of him was some nettle broth, a couple of goblets and a fine jug full of water. The man offered Fionn a bowl, poured him some water and then introduced himself. 'My name is Luachra.'

As Fionn sat down across from him, Luachra began talking. 'What is your name, young man, and what are you doing out so late at night?'

'My name is Fintan, and I have been travelling all day. I am a shepherd on my way to Connacht to find work after a summer on the Kerry mountains tending flocks. By the time I realised the sun had set, there was no sign of any homes I could call into. Your fire has been the first I've seen.'

'Just as well,' Luachra answered, smiling. 'It's not safe out here. Murderers and thieves roam these lands.'

'So I've heard,' Fionn replied. This remark made Luachra briefly eye him with suspicion before the moment passed and they began to eat in silence.

It wasn't until the meal was drawing to a close that Luachra, burping loudly, broke the silence. 'I feel like I have met you before?'

'I don't think so,' said Fionn. 'I've spent most of my life in the Scottish Highlands, where I moved when I was young. I am not long back home in Ireland, but

I am sure I would remember you if we had met.'

Luachra looked puzzled. 'Hmmm ... maybe I knew your father, then. What was his name?'

'Conleth,' said Fionn. 'He was also a shepherd.'

'Conleth the shepherd, eh?' Luachra smiled slyly, as if he knew something Fionn didn't. 'And where is Conleth the shepherd now?'

'He died when I was very young,' Fionn responded coldly. And for a moment it seemed that silence would again descend between them, but Luachra continued.

'Actually, I think I knew him. Yes, Conleth the shepherd, I met him many a time!'

Upon hearing this, anger grew in Fionn. This man, who was almost certainly a murderer and a thief, was provoking him. Most of Fionn's weapons were back with his travelling companions, but he had his knife sheathed and strapped to his side.

'I remember hearing that he had died. Killed by wolves while protecting his sheep, although his flock all died or disappeared in the end. At least, that's what I was told.'

Luachra looked Fionn directly in the eye, awaiting a reaction – but none came. Instead, Fionn answered, 'Yes, that's what I heard too.'

Luachra smiled. 'Right, enough sadness. I fancy ending the night with a game. Do you?' He took both goblets, stood up and walked around the fire to where he kept his belongings. His back was turned to Fionn. If Fionn chose, he could avenge the widow's loss in the same way her son was murdered – with a knife in the back. However, that was not the Fianna way, not his father's way, and it would not be Fionn's way. Luachra returned, holding two goblets that were filled with a liquid of a golden hue. He had three more goblets cradled under his arm – silver cups that matched the description Marga had given him of her stolen goblets.

'Here you go,' said Luachra, passing Fionn a goblet of golden liquid. 'Made to my own special recipe. Now, let me explain the game.' As he spoke, Luachra took the three empty goblets and placed them all upside down before turning the middle one back upright. 'In front of you sit three empty goblets. Three times you will turn two goblets with your hands. At the end of the third turn all goblets will face up towards the sky. You must do this quickly, without thinking and using only instinct and observation. I will show you how to do it first. What do you think?'

'I think they are nice goblets. Have you any more?'

Luachra smiled and looked across to his belongings. 'Yes, I have lots. I like to collect shiny things, especially gold and silver. It is amazing the things that you come across when you travel. Now, back to my game. You will have three turns to get it right. Every time you get it wrong, you must drink a mouthful from your goblet. If you empty your goblet before you manage to complete the task, I win, and you will gift me something.'

'Gift you what?'

'Oh, just something small. But if you win, you can keep all these fine goblets. Do you think you can do it?'

'Of course I can,' Fionn replied defiantly.

'All right then, first let me show you how to do it.' With great speed and deftness, Luachra took two goblets and flipped them. Then another two. And then two more. And in a flash, in three turns, all three goblets were now standing upright. 'Right, off you go,' he said, turning the middle goblet upside down again.

Fionn cracked his knuckles and got ready. 'One.' He flipped two cups. 'Two.' He flipped two cups. 'Three.' He flipped two cups. 'Oh!' Fionn blurted out. All of his goblets were flipped upside down!

'Drink,' Luachra shouted with glee. 'And watch properly this time!' He flipped the middle goblet once more and then made three quick moves. 'One ... two ... three!' All three goblets were now upright! 'Right, try again, young man,' he ordered, again turning the middle goblet upside down. But again when Fionn tried, the goblets all ended upside down.

'Drink!' cried Luachra, unable to hold back his delight. 'Boy, you are unable to follow Luachra's fast hands! Look again! One final time.' He flipped the middle goblet upright. Luachra went once more. 'One … two … three!'

Fionn looked astounded. Luachra had completed the exact same movements as he had, yet the goblets were again facing upright! Luachra smiled maliciously and flipped the middle goblet upside down once more for Fionn's last attempt. His goblet had only one mouthful left. Three times he had watched his opponent complete the task. But once more, much as he tried to mirror Luachra's movements, his final attempt left the goblets upside down. He would be forced to finish his drink, much to the elation of this tall, thin, villainous-looking man.

Luachra continued to laugh at Fionn's defeat until he saw Fionn holding his throat. 'What's wrong, boy?' he asked.

'I'm … fine … it's just … it's just …'

'Just what?'

'My throat … it feels … it's hard to breathe.' Suddenly, Fionn crumpled to the ground.

Luachra got up, walked around and stood over him. He seemed unconcerned – happy, in fact. 'Before you die on me, young man, there are three things you need to know. First, don't feel bad for not winning this little contest. My hands are the fastest in this land. You never stood a chance.'

'Second, that little something you will gift me is your little life. You see, your drink was extra special. It contained my own special ingredients of poisonous yew berries and toxic wild mushrooms. Don't worry, it will be all over soon. And finally, I did know your father. I knew him not as Conleth the shepherd but as Cumhall, the hopeless head of the Fianna. I guess that means you are Fionn Mac Cumhaill. And I am sure that there are many people who will be happy when I bring them your head. I think that is something worth celebrating, don't you think?'

Luachra picked up his own drink and looked down on Fionn, whose eyes were now closed as he drifted away. 'A toast to celebrate, I think? But who or what will I toast to? To your useless father, Cumhall? To finding one of his long-lost sheep? Or to me? Yes, I think it should be a toast to me.' Luachra then downed his goblet in one go.

With Fionn's eyes closed and his body no longer moving, Luachra returned to his belongings. He would need a good sharp axe to take Fionn's head off. After all, carrying a body back to Goll Mac Morna would be far too much trouble, especially when his bags were already full of stolen silver and golden treasures. As he searched for his axe, Luachra thought he could feel the slightest sensation of dryness in his own throat – a dryness that soon began to tighten. He turned around and there in front of him, holding two goblets, was Fionn!

'Before you die, Luachra, there are three things you need to know,' a very much alive Fionn announced. 'First, I don't feel too bad for losing that contest, but you were wrong. Your hands are not the fastest in this land.' And with that, Fionn switched and spun the goblets between his hands with such speed and deftness that a cold chill ran down Luachra's spine. He now realised that Fionn had swapped their drinks when his greed made him turn around to look at his stolen treasures.

'Second, I knew you had poisoned my drink. You were unarmed, so how else were you going to murder a stranger you had just welcomed? I knew that is what you would do, just like you murdered Lonán and every other poor victim you stole this gold and silver from. And finally, I don't know how you knew my father, Cumhall, but he was neither hopeless nor useless. He was a hero who protected his flock until the day he died. And now one of those lost sheep is coming home.'

And with that, Luachra's eyes closed and he breathed his last.

• • •

In the darkness, the three siblings saw a figure draw near. They unsheathed their swords but quickly realised it was Fionn and rushed forward to welcome him. Fionn told them what had happened, and when he reached the end of his tale, he passed them Luachra's bag of riches.

'These three goblets belong to your aunt. Bring them back to her. For the rest, I trust you to return them to their rightful owners. There is only one thing I am taking with me – this oxter bag.' Fionn produced a bag of leather that he hung on his shoulder. 'I cannot open it,' he continued, 'but something tells me it belongs close to me.'

As the first slivers of dawn slid along the eastern horizon, the siblings and Fionn wished each other well and went their separate ways.

• • •

Crimmal, son of Trenmor, brother of Cumhall, uncle of Fionn, sat down to rest his weary legs. He looked around. Sharing with him in what had been the yield of another poor hunt were the remnants of Clan Bascna. It was many years ago now that they had left the service of Conn of the Hundred Battles, High King of Ireland. They had suffered several attacks from the forces of Goll Mac Morna. The last of those attacks had been a few years ago. Since then, they had retreated to the deepest recesses of Connemara, to live their lives free of their enemies. However, in a woodland surrounded by marshes, mountains and moors, game was in short supply. To make matters worse, the constant damp meant that they could not always create a fire to stay warm through a winter's evening. Crimmal could see in the faces of his men that these hard years had taken their toll. They were once a fighting force, but now they were mere shadows of their former selves, fighting only to survive and nothing more.

Like an apparition, a young man entered their circle. Believing him to be an assassin sent by Goll to kill their leader and scatter the rest of them to the wind, they drew their rusted swords, spears and axes. But Crimmal knew immediately who this young boy was.

'Demne!' he called.

Fionn could not remember when he had last been called by that name. He turned to see a man with tear-filled eyes approaching him. 'Uncle Crimmal!'

They embraced. A joy that Crimmal had not felt for a long, long time washed over him. Crimmal then introduced Fionn to his men and they shared stories of the history that had separated them since Fionn's birth at the Battle of Cnucha. Fionn had brought food with him and they had a feast, for it was not every day that a family was reunited.

Fionn told them about his adventures and finally shared his most recent. However, he had only begun telling them about Luachra when Crimmal interrupted.

'The Grey of Luachra!'

'Yes, that's him. He said he knew Cumhall.'

'He knew all of us,' Crimmal replied. 'He was once the treasurer of the Fianna who guarded our riches – but gold and silver corrupted his heart. It was he who dealt Cumhall the blow that lead to your father's death at the Battle of Cnucha. And for his betrayal of Cumhall, Goll rewarded him with your father's magic treasure bag.'

Fionn's eyes opened wide. 'Magic? What does this magic treasure bag look like?' As Crimmal began to describe it, Fionn took out the oxter bag he had taken from Luachra.

'That's it!' cried Crimmal. 'That's Cumhall's treasure bag!'

Holding it in his hands, Crimmal shared the history of this extraordinary bag. 'The tale of this treasure bag starts at the time of Manannán Mac Lir, God of the Sea, who was one of the Tuatha Dé Danaan. The Tuatha were a supernatural race who lived on this island long before the first mortals arrived. When men and women appeared on these shores, many of the Tuatha Dé Danaan took the form of humans and interacted with them – sometimes for good, sometimes for bad.

'Manannán Mac Lir had a son, Ilbrach, who fell in love with a strong-willed young woman called Aoife. However, it was forbidden for any of the Tuatha Dé Danaan to form a relationship with these newly arrived people, and although Aoife loved him back, she feared retribution from the gods and rejected his advances. Ilbrach was heartbroken and went back into the sea. For months, Atlantic showers drenched the coast of Donegal where Aoife lived. More than anything, Manannán Mac Lir wanted his son to be happy, and when he finally discovered the reason for his son's sorrow, he visited Aoife one dark and miserable day. Manannán pleaded with her to cast aside her fear because he, the God of the Sea, promised to protect all mortals and assured her they would come to no harm. Finally, Aoife accepted, and she and Ilbrach formed a loving union.

'However, not all the Tuatha Dé Danaan were happy with what had been allowed to happen. Chief among them was Uis, a goddess of the water who wanted Ilbrach for herself. She waited until one day when Manannán and Ilbrach were far out to sea to trick Aoife into entering the water by telling her Ilbrach was waiting there to surprise her. Once in the goddess's aquatic domain, Aoife was turned into a crane. Her wings were weak and she lacked the strength to withstand the strong Atlantic winds, so she was driven far inland, cursed to fly from lough to lough.

'When Ilbrach returned, he was told that Uis had lured Aoife into the water. Believing that she had drowned, he could not be consoled and grew wild and fierce with anger, slaying Uis before departing for the sea — never to return. It was said that for two hundred years he was a tempest that blew far out in the ocean. No matter how many times Manannán tried to bring him back to shore, Ilbrach never returned. Eventually, he perished of sadness and exhaustion. In tribute, Manannán created a full month of sun with no wind or rain along the coast of Donegal, making it the most beautiful place this world has ever seen. It was during this time that a crane appeared on the cliffs, and it didn't move from the ocean's edge for the entire month. Manannán knew that there must be a reason for the crane's presence. He felt in his heart that the crane and his son had a special bond. When the month came to an end, he ordered a window in his castle to be left open throughout the year so that the crane could take shelter if an Atlantic storm came crashing in. A year after his son died, Manannán heard that the crane had entered his castle through this window a few days before in fine weather, but it had not yet left.

'Worried, he knocked down the door to the room where the crane sheltered. And there, lying on the floor, was Aoife, now an old woman who looked close to death. On the ground beside her lay the body of the dead crane she had finally cast off. She told Manannán what had happened to her, and he begged for forgiveness. Before she passed away, she told him that his promise to protect men and women was no longer enough and demanded that he should gift them a treasure bag that a leader could always call upon to keep themselves and their people safe from harm, wherever it might come from. Manannán promised that he would. When Aoife died, he took the lifeless body of the crane, which she had inhabited for two hundred years, and made a bag from it. He put his own knife and shield in it and then travelled around the seas of neighbouring islands, filling it with the best weapons and armour he could find. He took the King of Scotland's shears, the King of Norway's horned helmet, a mystical belt made of a strip of whale skin, a Galician sling and many more magical items.

'The bag had the potential to cause great harm, so Manannán put a charm on the bag – it could only be opened by the most virtuous and just. It is unclear through whose hands it passed, but it finally came to your father and remained with him until the Grey of Luachra stole it.'

After Crimmal finished, he looked at Fionn with eyes that suddenly seemed years younger and said, 'Your return to us and the return of this treasure bag means that the prophecy must be true. It said that one day our clan – Clan Bascna – would become leaders of the Fianna once again and rid it of the decay that is currently destroying it.'

Fionn nodded but then said timidly, 'But I must not be virtuous or just – I can't open the treasure bag.'

Crimmal smiled. 'It has one last charm. Even for the most virtuous, it opens only when it needs to be opened – in battle.'

'Well, we need to get ready for battle then,' Fionn replied.

• • •

For the next month, Fionn, Crimmal and their men began venturing out further from their place of refuge. They found more food, honed their fighting skills and readied themselves for the battles that lay ahead. Crimmal told Fionn stories of his father and his mother, and upon hearing tales of his parents, Fionn became even more determined to overthrow Goll Mac Morna and become leader of the Fianna as his father had once been. He knew the time for hiding was nearly at an end. And the time for defeating evil was about to begin. But something gnawed at Fionn. Crimmal could see this. One evening, after they had eaten, he sat down with Fionn.

'You don't feel ready, do you?' Crimmal asked.

'I feel stronger, fitter and more determined than ever – but something is missing.'

Crimmal nodded. 'You're right. If you want to set out for Tara tomorrow to battle Goll and his men, we are ready to follow you. However, if you want to be a true champion and leader to the Fianna, one whom everyone will look up to, you need to learn one more skill. You have shown bravery in battle and are unmatched in the hunt, but what you lack is the art of poetry. Unless you master this skill, you will only ever be as brutish as Goll and will never be a true leader.'

Fionn nodded, realising that this was the last piece of the puzzle he had been looking for. 'But how can I become a great poet?'

'Finnegas,' Crimmal said. 'You need to find Finnegas. He will teach you. And when that is done, we will be ready, my nephew.'

THE SALMON OF KNOWLEDGE

'**G**reat Abcán!' roared the old man.

From where he squatted, Fionn could see the small bearded figure sway and teeter and then tumble out of his little boat and into the water with a large splash. Fionn went to step out from the bushes where he hid. They were in the depths of winter and the river was icy cold. But before Fionn could move, the little man had already resurfaced, cursing his bad luck as his fishing rod floated fast downstream. He dragged his soaked body back into this boat and was still swearing as he pulled up an anchor and began rowing to shore.

As the old man stepped onto dry land Fionn wondered whether this really was the man whom his uncle Crimmal

had spoken about — the great Finnegas, legendary Celtic poet. It was said that Finnegas could recall poetry from as far back as the Muintir Cessair, the first inhabitants of Ireland. Indeed, people learned of these creatures — part-spirit, part-mortal and part-legend — from the poems that Finnegas held on to in his head. Such was Finnegas's knowledge of rhyme and verse that Crimmal used say that Finnegas knew more poetry than every other druid in Ireland. But Fionn didn't see a famed poet. He saw a small, shivering, bedraggled old man with a weather-beaten face and snow-white beard, who was soaking wet and swearing a lot. Yet this was where Crimmal had said Finnegas's camp would be — deep in the Forbidden Forest, on the banks of the River Boyne.

'Hello,' Fionn called as he stepped out from the trees. If the old man was surprised at the boy's sudden appearance, he didn't show it. In fact, when Fionn tried to introduce himself to the old man, Finnegas cut him off and instructed him to bring some of the dry wood that had been stored a little distance away. Fionn did as he was asked, and the old man stoked the glowing embers, bringing the fire back to life to warm his shivering limbs.

'You'll need to get some more wood,' said Fionn as he sat down across from him. 'You'll soon run out.'

'Aye,' the old man replied. 'I am always running low on firewood. I'll put it on my to-do list.'

The warmth of the flames seemed to relax the old man and soon a contented smile spread across his face. He looked over at Fionn. Fionn noticed that there was something about his eyes that was a little different. His right eye looked at Fionn directly, but the left eye stared off into the middle distance as if he were deep in thought.

'You must be Fionn?'

'How did you know?'

'You have your father's face and your mother's eyes. I've been expecting you for quite some time now.'

'Are you Finnegas?'

'Yes, I am he. I was beginning to wonder if you would ever come find me.'

'How did you know that I would try?'

'I'm a poet,' Finnegas answered with a smile, 'and poetry is not just about entertaining and telling stories of what has happened. Sometimes it is about telling stories of what will — or might — happen.'

'I don't understand?'

'Of course you don't. You haven't learned anything yet. But don't worry — you soon will. If you want to become the heroic leader of the Fianna, the champion whom all will look up to, whom poems will be written about, then we have much to learn and little time to do it. We'll start tomorrow. Tonight, you must rest.'

• • •

The next morning, bright and early, as the subtle aroma of their breakfast of mushroom broth still filled the air, Finnegas began to teach Fionn how to become a great poet.

'Have you anything you want to ask, my boy, before we commence our learning?'

'I have a couple of questions.'

'Go ahead.'

'Why poetry? Why is it important that true warriors know poetry?'

'Our poetry is not just words that rhyme. It is much more than that,' Finnegas replied. 'It's what helps us understand the history that came before, so we can understand the future that lies ahead. It helps us remember those who walked this land many moons ago and those who walk it today. Poetry is the wealth of true Fianna warriors. It is what keeps you on the right path, and it shields you from corruption and greed.'

Fionn's expression betrayed his confusion.

'You see, Fionn, power that is left unchecked always corrupts — always. When mere mortals hold absolute power, a thirst grows. It is a thirst for wealth — the wealth of cattle, of land, of gold, of more power. It is a thirst that is hard to quench. The warrior's real wealth is his knowledge of verse and this is the purest and fairest form of wealth because once it is created and spoken it is shared by all in the community. It gains value over time and can never be taken from you. That is why it is so important.'

'I have one more question.'

'Speak.'

'Who's Abcán?' Fionn enquired.

'Who?'

'Abcán,' Fionn repeated. 'You called out his name as you were falling into the river yesterday.'

Finnegas grinned, realising Fionn had seen him fall off the boat. 'Abcán was a poet and musician. He was said to be smaller in size than even me but was recognised as the greatest of his kind in the time of the Tuatha Dé Danann, the tribe of gods that once ruled these lands.'

'I have heard of the Tuatha. They were the first settlers of this land, weren't they?' said Fionn.

'They were among the first settlers,' Finnegas corrected him. 'There were stories of others, but it was the Tuatha who put their stamp on this island before all others. However, other tribes were living here when the Tuatha arrived. The strongest were the Fir Bolg, but the Tuatha soon defeated them. The Tuatha then overcame the Fomorians, who had risen up from the sea to try to take this island.'

At the mention of the Fomorians, Fionn felt a pang of sadness as he remembered his friends Gobán, Garb and Gadra, and their killing at the hands of Beirgín, the giant of Fomorian blood. It was not yet two springtimes ago, but already it seemed so distant.

'After a long time ruling this land,' Finnegas continued, 'and planting the seeds of magic, myth and legend in her soil, the Tuatha would do battle once more with a new race of people. This time it was the Milesians, a great wave of men and women that came up from a land far to the south of this island. In truth, they could have lived together in peace because the Milesians didn't want war, but the Tuatha had become set in their ways and were unwilling to accommodate these new arrivals. The Milesians were, of course, not going to turn back. Only Abcán spoke out against conflict. He went to Mac Cecht, Mac Cuill and Mac Gréine, who were the kings of the Tuatha at the time, and recited verse after verse. In his poetry he presented both the history and the future of Ireland, a future that would witness tides of people wash in and out over this land. He alone argued that the Milesians should be welcomed as we welcome the high tide.'

'What happened?' Fionn asked, engrossed in the story.

'They didn't listen. They spurned the wisdom of the poet, and a great battle took place that killed many and injured more. After a week of fierce fighting, the kings of the Tuatha asked for a truce. During this time the Milesians agreed to stay aboard their ships and lay anchor nine waves' distance from the shore. For three days, the druids and priests of both sides gathered the bodies of their fallen warriors and bade farewell to them. For the Tuatha, this meant ferrying their dead to the Otherworld aboard a boat made of bronze with a tin sail. It was Abcán who navigated the boat from this world to the next.

'While he was gone on this journey, Mac Cecht, Mac Cuill and Mac Gréine oversaw the formation of a magical storm that they hoped would drive the Milesians away. The Milesians would have been dashed against the rocks had it not been for their own great poet, Amhairghin, who calmed the seas with his verse. The Milesians were enraged that a sacred truce had been broken. In a bout of fury, they inflicted untold damage on the Tuatha Dé Danann.

'When Abcán arrived back from the Otherworld, he was met with devastation. He could see the Tuatha Dé Danann were heading for destruction and pleaded with the kings to ask for peace, which they at first refused to consider. They would rather see the destruction of their people than give up their home. Finally, Abcán and Amhairghin came up with a plan for peace to which all sides agreed. The terms of the plan were clear: they would drop all of their weapons, announce that no one had been the victor and name the land after the wives of the three Tuatha kings – Éire, Banba and Fódla, although it was the name of the youngest of these wives, Éire, that was used most frequently.'

Fionn looked puzzled. He knew that the Tuatha no longer roamed the land, even if their names had remained.

'But,' Finnegas continued, 'at the last moment, King Mac Cecht insisted that he would not share the land with these new settlers and instead the island should be split in half. To everyone's surprise, Amhairghin agreed. He asked only that he could choose the Milesians' half first and that the three kings would swear by their most sacred of oaths that they would accept his choice.'

'What happened? Which half did Amhairghin choose? The north or south? East or west?'

'He chose all of them,' Finnegas laughed.

'Huh?'

'Amhairghin tricked them. He chose the world above ground for the Milesians, and he sent the Tuatha to the world below ground – the Otherworld. The kings rose up in protest, but this time the rest of the Tuatha rose up against them. To break their most sacred of oaths would mean eternal damnation for them, so they chose a new leader – Manannán Mac Lir. It was he who said goodbye to the land of Éire and led the Tuatha Dé Danann to the Otherworld. Only Abcán, who had tried to achieve peace and reconcile both sides, was allowed to step foot into this world.'

'That's some story,' said Fionn.

'Now, young Fionn, understanding a story is one thing, but being able to tell it is another.' And with that, Finnegas recounted this tale once more but did so in verse, in such a way that the tales of Abcán, Amhairghin, the Tuatha and the Milesians came alive in his mind.

● ● ●

Over the next few weeks, starting at daybreak each day, Finnegas would teach Fionn the history of Ireland and how it could be told through verse. In the afternoons, he would leave Fionn alone to recite the poems to himself. Fionn was an exceptional learner. Sometimes he only had to hear a poem once to be able to recall it. By the time Finnegas returned from his fishing trips, Fionn would often be able to recount the poems he learnt that morning word for word. Fionn would then hunt and forage in the forest for their meals, a time he particularly enjoyed. It was a time to wander and remember when he was that bit younger and everything seemed like an adventure to be enjoyed. Of late, Fionn had started to feel the weight on his shoulders of something he could not yet put a name to. He missed having someone his own age to share this burden with. Getting out into the wide woodland wilderness was always a welcome comfort.

Soon Finnegas moved from explaining the events in these poems to the wisdom and meaning that many contained. They discussed this late each evening over supper. This food was almost always prepared by Fionn, partly to thank Finnegas for all his help and partly because Fionn's meals were altogether more sumptuous than the stodgy stews Finnegas produced. One evening, their conversation turned to the topic of food.

'Finnegas?'

'Yes,' the old man replied. 'What is it?'

'Every morning you teach me more poems and every day I am more impressed by the depth of your knowledge. But if you don't mind me saying, I'm less impressed by your fishing skills. I mean, don't get me wrong, I'm happy to hunt, gather and cook. I enjoy it. But every afternoon you go out fishing and all you ever come back with are baby fish.' To help explain his point, Fionn held out one such example he had found hiding in the stew.

'I would never kill a baby fish!' Finnegas interjected. 'You should never kill baby fish! Otherwise, you won't have any adults who will have their own baby fish when they get older. What you are holding is a pinkeen.'

'A pinkeen? What on earth is that?'

'It's a very, very small adult fish.'

Fionn looked at what he was holding as if some great secret had been revealed. 'Apologies. Every afternoon you go out fishing and all you come back with are very, very small adult fish.'

'And what is your question?'

'Do you think it might be time to change the bait you use to catch fish? Each morning you pocket a few hazelnuts to put on the end of your line, so I'm not surprised you catch only pinkeens. Why not use the pinkeens instead? You have silver ones, copper ones and greenbacks. They're great for catching bigger fish — bream, perch and pike. Sure, even a few worms will catch you a trout.'

'But I'm not looking to catch bream, perch, pike or trout.'

'What are you trying to catch?'

'A salmon,' Finnegas replied.

'In winter? Sure, salmon don't begin making their runs up the rivers until spring.'

'But this isn't any old salmon. This one is special.'

Finnegas then recounted the tale of the most famous fish that had ever lived — the Salmon of Knowledge.

'It began back when the Tuatha Dé Danann were forced to leave these lands for the Otherworld. The

Tuatha were sometimes known as the Folk of the Danu – Danu was a goddess of nature. They had become the guardians of this earth on behalf of Danu and they swore to always look after it. They tended the soil with great care and respect and sowed it with ten thousand shades of green. However, when they were forced to depart this land for the Otherworld, they left it all behind for the Milesians. But the Milesians struggled to live in harmony with nature and knew little in the ways of minding it.

'After some time, Abcán began coming back from his journeys with stories of what was happening to Éire. There were many tales of how the Milesians neglected rather than nurtured. There was an account of one tribe in the westerly land of Clare that had allowed their cattle to graze every blade of grass, turning the land to rock and stone.

'The Tuatha lamented the destruction and decided that, as much as they might loathe the Milesians for making them exiles, the knowledge of how to care for the earth needed to be passed from one world to the next. There were those who argued against them. Some, still filled with self-pity and pride, swore that they would never help the people who had taken their home. Others believed the Milesians could not be trusted and would use the knowledge for their own corrupt ends. However, in the end, the Tuatha decided that they would transfer their wisdom to the land of the Milesians through the roots of trees.

'Seven types of tree were chosen — oak, pine, ash, yew, holly, hazel and apple. Soon, the learned people of the Milesians — the poets and druids — found peace and understanding in the presence of these trees. Recognising this strange gift, the Milesians chose to protect these types of tree and gave them the name "Airig Fedo" — the lords of the wood — which is why it is still a crime before the High King to cut any of these down.

'Of all these trees, one specimen stood out. High on a hilltop near the centre of this island, an old hazel overlooked a small pool of water that became known as the Well of Wisdom. It was a steep climb to find it, but, once there, the insights received in its presence outshone those rewarded by every other tree. One spring, nine hazelnuts grew on its branches. These hazelnuts remained ripe all year round, and it was rumoured that they would give the person who ate them all the knowledge in the world.

'Soon every druid and poet was insisting that they alone should eat these hazelnuts. Arguments broke out as many so-called learned men, along with warriors to back them, came to this tree to claim its fruit. However, just as it seemed that there would be bloodshed, a small old bearded man with wet feet wandered through the angry crowd unnoticed. Stopping at the pool close to the branch from which the hazelnuts grew, he took a small spear from beneath his cloak and, with a flick of his wrist, fired it at the fruit. The nine hazelnuts were severed from the tree and fell into the water below. As the poets and druids turned around in shock, a speckled salmon that had been swimming lazily in the well gobbled them up before disappearing into the depths, just like the old man, who vanished in the commotion.'

'Abcán?' Fionn interrupted, grinning.

'Yes, Abcán,' came the reply. 'That was the last that anyone saw of the fish that became known as the Salmon of Knowledge.'

'Then what?' Fionn asked.

'Then somehow your grandfather Tadg discovered that a magical fish swam in this stretch of the River Boyne.'

'My grandfather?' Fionn gasped.

'Yes, your grandfather Tadg. Do you recognise this place?' Finnegas said cryptically.

'No.'

'Are you sure?'

Fionn hesitated before speaking. 'Sometimes in the forest I see trees and groves that look familiar, but I have never been here before — so how could I recognise them?'

'Because your mother passed these visions on to you. You see, your mother, Muirne, grew up in the nearby

now-abandoned palace of Almu but would escape at any chance she got and spend all her time in this forest, away from her wicked father — your grandfather. In fact, this is where she spent the only happy moments of her childhood. In the twenty years before your birth, these forests were all but forbidden. Few could enter here. Only the Fianna were allowed in to hunt and no one was allowed to fish.'

'Because of the Salmon of Knowledge?'

'That's right. How Tadg knew that the salmon lived here I have never found out, but I suspect it has something to do with the dark magic that changed him from the kindly, wise young man I once knew to the evil, angry druid he became. Thankfully, he never caught the fish, and the High King forced him to give up these lands, including Almu, when he got rid of him. I heard about Tadg's fruitless search from those who had the misfortune to serve under him. And I have been visiting here ever since, trying to catch this fish.'

After a while, Fionn asked about his evil grandfather. 'Is he dead?'

'No one really knows. But I have heard rumours that an old man who looks like him has been spotted near sidhe mounds that have been disturbed and whose spirits have been released.'

'I slew one of those spirits in Kerry,' Fionn said.

'It was good practice for the dragon, then.'

166

'Dragon?' Fionn exclaimed. 'What dragon?'

'You really have been living down a hole if you haven't heard of the dragon!' Finnegas said. 'For more than a year now, every new moon when the skies are dark, a fire-breathing dragon named Aillen Mac Miona has swept across the land, terrorising the High King's home of Tara, reducing large parts of it to ash and killing and injuring many people. Every month, the High King, his men and the Fianna have tried to face it, but every month they have failed ...' Finnegas trailed off.

Fionn could see that something had just occurred to the old poet. 'What is it?'

'If you didn't know about the dragon, then I fear you didn't hear about your mother.'

Fionn looked down as he felt hot tears come to his eyes. Finnegas hugged him and was silent as Fionn grieved the mother he had met only once, whom he would have to wait until the next world to meet again. When the tears dried, Finnegas told him that Muirne was among the dragon's first victims and, from what he had been told, she had felt no pain.

An hour passed before Fionn finally spoke again. 'I will honour her as I will honour my father – by continuing with my quest. And I believe that the wisdom you will gain from eating the salmon will help me, so let's try to catch it.'

'Have you any idea how we can do this?'

'Well, you won't get to eat him if you keep using hazelnuts as bait. You don't have to be wise to know that it is the stupid man who does the same thing over and over but expects to get a different result.'

'So, what do you suggest?'

Fionn looked off in the direction of the river for a moment. 'We change the menu.'

Over the next month, Fionn grew more focused than ever. He continued to learn every morning, before spending the afternoon hunting and gathering. Finnegas continued with his fishing expeditions, trying out new forms of bait Fionn developed. They tried various woodland grubs, black truffles from the woodland floor and every other sort of mushroom. They even tried smelly stinkhorns but stopped using them when Finnegas caught a pike that nearly chewed his ankle off! When they had tried every type of bait he could find on land, Fionn turned to the woodland streams for ideas. He started with crayfish before turning to freshwater shrimp. There were several weeks of trial and error (mostly error), and they were starting to think that the salmon was either not hungry or not even at home.

But one day, when Fionn was searching for new bait, he heard a call ring through the woods.

'Fionn! Fionn! FIONN!'

Fionn could hear his name being called from deep in the dark forest. It was Finnegas. And it sounded like trouble. He threw down that afternoon's woodland bounty and bounded towards the shouts, drawing his dagger from its sheath. But as he burst into the clearing of Finnegas's home, instead of being met by Goll or a band of thieves, he was greeted by Finnegas holding the most enormous salmon Fionn had ever seen.

'That's some pinkeen,' Fionn joked.

'This is no pinkeen. This here is the Salmon of Knowledge! We're having fish for dinner!' Finnegas said as he laid the salmon down and began rekindling the fire.

'I'll get some more firewood,' said Fionn.

'No, I will. I've waited seven years to taste this fish and I am not going to ruin it by burning it. You're the cook. But remember, whatever you do —'

'Don't eat any of it, because the first person who eats the salmon will receive all its wisdom,' Fionn said. 'You need not worry. I won't eat one tiny bit.'

In a very short time, the fire was roaring again. As the flames rose, Fionn skewered the fish and set it high enough above the fire that it didn't burn but close enough that it soon began to cook. He slowly rotated the skewer, and the smell of roasting salmon soon filled the air. Fionn thought that some fresh herbs might go well with the meal. Leaving the fish for a moment, he ran to a spot nearby where wild sorrel grew. However, by the time he returned with the herbs, he saw that a blister had formed on the fish where it had been left over the flames for a moment too long.

At first, he let it be, but on each rotation the blister grew. Fionn reached across to puncture it with his thumb.

'Ow!'

'What is it?' said Finnegas, who had just arrived back to the camp with firewood. He laid the wood down and approached Fionn, but his look of concern turned to alarm when he saw him sucking his thumb. Something in the boy looked so different.

'I went to get some herbs, and when I returned a blister had formed on the fish. It kept growing bigger, so I went to burst it —'

'And it burnt your thumb?'

Fionn saw the fear on the old man's face. 'I didn't eat anything. I just burnt my thumb and ...'

But at that moment they both knew. Fionn could feel a greater sense of awareness coursing through his veins. He was still a boy, but he now felt older. Finnegas saw it in his eyes and the dread the old man had felt melted into relief. Maybe this was why it had taken him so long to catch the salmon.

'I'm sorry, Finnegas,' Fionn whispered.

'Don't be,' the old poet replied. 'It makes sense that

it is you who has this wisdom. After all, if you succeed in your attempt to lead the Fianna, you will need to be wise beyond your years to steer them through the years ahead. Now, you must return to Crimmal and the rest of your kinsmen in the west. You must gather as many people as you can to aid and protect you against Goll and his men. And then you need to return to Tara and become the champion of the Fianna – that is your destiny.'

As Fionn looked at the ground, saddened that once again he was to bid goodbye to another friend, Finnegas continued. 'Don't feel too downhearted, it could be worse – you could have burnt it. Now, you better finish cooking it so we can eat. You'll need strength as well as wisdom for what lies ahead.'

THE DRAGON OF TARA

'Q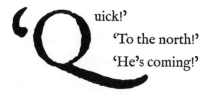uick!'

        'To the north!'

        'He's coming!'

'Take cover!'

'Hide!'

As shouts, roars and screams filled the air around Tara, Fiacha took the spear that his old friend Cumhall had given him many years ago. It was almost two decades since Cumhall had fled with Muirne, allowing the monstrous Goll to take over as leader of the Fianna. Fiacha had been sent, along with Crimmal, Luchet and Dúnán, to give Cumhall an ultimatum — return or face death. When both Cumhall and Muirne refused to come back, Fiacha had wanted to stay with them. But Cumhall needed him to return.

'Go back, my friend. Tell the High King that we're sorry but our answer is no. Keep a close eye on him and protect him from harm.' Cumhall then gave him this spear. 'Hold on to this for me. Putting it to your forehead will grant the holder resolve and the steadfastness of the immoveable mountain peaks. One day it will be needed to defend our kingdom from a danger greater than you or I can possibly know.'

In the years that followed, Fiacha had felt that he had let his old friend down. He had tried to keep a close eye on the High King, but he had been powerless to prevent the Fianna becoming an increasingly disorderly group. Many of their number were now rumoured to use their power to bully and harass the people they had sworn to protect. He was also powerless to prevent Goll and his followers from attacking the remaining forces of Clan Bascna out west and from chasing the shadow of Cumhall's son.

But Fiacha could not be too hard on himself. He had counselled Conn of the Hundred Battles to get rid of the evil druid Tadg, had spent many productive years helping Conn's son Art to grow into a wise young boy and had held on to the magic spear that Cumhall had left him. And now he knew why it was so important. It might be the only form of defence against the dragon that was fast approaching them!

Every month for over a year now, the birth of a new moon had brought with it an evil spirit in the shape of a dragon that terrorised Tara. The dragon had begun its attacks during the feast of Samhain, a time of year when fairy folk, spirits and the descendants of the Tuatha Dé Danann tried to re-enter the world of mortals through sidhe mounds like the one that the wild boar of Torc Mountain had emerged from.

At first it seemed that there was no way to stand up to the dragon. As it neared, it sang a magical song of such enchantment and charm that even the bravest of warriors protecting the old stronghold were entranced into a deep sleep, lying motionless as the dragon breathed great flames that set many of the buildings of the ancient capital alight.

On that first occasion it killed many and destroyed anything in its way. Every month since, it had returned, sending the royal family, warriors and inhabitants of Tara fleeing for the woods. There they cowered together as the dragon heaped more ruin upon their homes, cattle and food supplies.

Fiacha had come to understand the true magic of the spear. Holding it to his forehead had created the sense of resolve that Cumhall had spoken about, making him immune to the dragon's song. However, he had never been able to get close enough to throw it at the dragon. On the one occasion he did get close, the dragon saw him and he had barely escaped with his life. While he still held on to the spear, hope had loosened its grip on him. He feared that the Kingdom of Tara was nearing its end.

• • •

As he heard the first faint strains of the dragon's song and felt drowsiness creeping into his bones, Goll too quickened his pace so he would reach the cover of the woods before sleep took over. The king, his son Art and the people of Tara left their houses with as much food as they could carry for the distant safety of the forest. Having made sure everyone had followed the High King's orders to leave, Goll and his men were now taking their positions a safe distance from the capital as the dragon drew near.

These enchanted sleeps were not happy ones for Goll. For over a year now, he had been powerless to prevent ruin befalling Tara. He knew that Conn was disappointed in him. To add to his woes, the hunt for Cumhall's son had failed. Fionn escaped his grasp time after time. And now there were stories from the west of a fair-haired boy with a maturity beyond his years raising an army to march on Tara. As his eyes closed and he drifted off, Goll knew his time was running out

• • •

Cana awoke to what sounded like thunder. She sprang up from where she had lain and peeked outside her shelter. From this place of rest on the side of Slieve Fuad, a two-day hike west of her home in Donard, Cana saw only the silvery Armagh countryside that spread out beneath them, illuminated by a clear starry sky. No thunder without clouds, she thought.

'What was that, little sister?' Iollan asked.

'I don't know, but we're not the only ones who heard it,' she answered, nodding to the rest of their group, who had also woken up. 'Grab a sword and come with me.'

Together, Cana and her brother scrambled up the eastern face of the mountain to the summit. As Iollan clambered to keep up, he smiled with pride at his young sister. Since Fionn had left them, she had become more than just captain of the hurlers of Donard. It turned out that she was a born leader who all the community now looked to. So, when local poets began to recite verses telling of a boy named Fionn who was calling on those who supported a return to peace, calm and prosperity to come to his aid, Cana called on both boys and girls to join her in fighting for him. Iollan and many others were quick to do so.

Reaching the summit, they scoured the Armagh countryside that surrounded them, but saw nothing apart from the entrance to a sidhe mound.

'Do you think it was fairy folk?' Iollan asked.

'Maybe. Very noisy fairy folk if it was,' Cana answered. 'Come on, let's return and tell everyone to go back to sleep. We'll be up again in just a couple of hours and we have several days of marching before we reach Connemara.'

• • •

Conn walked into what had once been the Great Banqueting Hall, an enormous building that had held feasts which lasted for days. It had been nearly three weeks since the last assault by the dragon, yet he could still smell smouldering oak in the air. The first time the dragon had come from the north, it had set this great structure ablaze, burning it to the ground. It was one building that Conn had never rebuilt. To have feasts while his home was being terrorised by this evil spirit would not be right. Instead, every time the dragon laid waste to other parts of Tara, the king redoubled his efforts to have those parts rebuilt.

At least no one had lost their life this time. Small mercies. Still, he realised that things were only getting worse. But although he had not yet come up with a way to kill the dragon, he couldn't let it destroy Tara. Every month he tried to rebuild. But it was becoming a fruitless task and one his subjects were beginning to tire of. Once, it had only been his closest advisors who told him that he should abandon Tara, but he now heard these conversations everywhere – his subjects no longer cared who heard them. Indeed, many had already left to seek refuge elsewhere.

Although many of those who had departed did so because of the now-monthly attacks, there were some who had heard of a fair-haired boy called Fionn, who was gathering warriors to march on Tara. It was the worry of what this invasion would bring that made staying in the area too much for some. Conn was worried too. He had allowed Goll to search for this young boy since the child had been born. The High King knew what Goll would do if he found Fionn. As he looked at his own son, Art, who was only a little younger than the boy, he felt a deep sense of shame for letting Goll chase after him for so long. Now he feared that Fionn was coming to Tara for revenge.

• • •

At that very moment, in the heart of Connemara, Fionn was thinking not of revenge but of the dragon and how he might defeat it.

'Strange habit you've picked up,' Crimmal said, bringing Fionn out of his reverie.

'What?'

'Sucking your thumb. Most people bite their nails when they're nervous.'

'I'm not nervous,' Fionn said. 'I was just thinking.'

'Well, I can come back if you want.'

'No, it's all right. What is it?'

'More warriors are joining our ranks.'

'Where are they?' Fionn asked. Since Fionn had put out a call to arms, his army had swelled. Many people could no longer accept the rule of the High King and the disorder that his Fianna warriors continued to cause.

'She said she's been travelling some distance and was wondering about the poor welcome for friends of Fionn.'

Fionn's face lit up. Only a few days ago, his friend Cnes had arrived with a contingent from the Kingdom of Aghadoe. The news that another female friend had arrived meant it could only be Cana from Donard. He ran to meet the new arrivals.

'My goodness, I would hardly recognise you.' Fionn greeted Cana with the warmest of embraces before hugging Iollan with equal enthusiasm. 'What happened to your hair?'

'I thought I should get it cut,' Cana replied. 'I reckoned that tucking loose strands behind my ear every time I went to puck a sideline ball was one thing – fixing my hair in the heat of battle was another.'

'Well, I thank you from the bottom of my heart for cutting it – and for coming to our aid.'

'We are happy to serve under you again,' Cana said, 'but there is no need to thank us. We come to your aid, but we are also here to come to this island's aid. The great darkness that has been hanging over our land needs to be lifted. We want to play our part in achieving this.'

• • •

That evening, surrounded by friends, family and fellow warriors from the length and breadth of Ireland, Fionn began his address.

'For far too long the island of Ireland has been under a cloud. Since the murder of my father, the High King and the Fianna have led this country astray. Families are afraid that their huts will be broken into at night. Men and women have been killed as they moved from one village to the next. Tombs have been raided and disturbed, releasing spirits that are looking for revenge. Whole lands have gone hungry. And many settlements have been destroyed by thieves and outlaws. Tomorrow we will march on Tara. Once there, we will demand change, or we will make this change ourselves. Who's with me?'

The answer came in the form of a hundred cheers.

The next day, they set out for Tara, marching eastwards as the spring days lengthened. From the hilly and boggy grounds of the west, through the flatter landscape of the midlands, across rivers great and small, they trooped unopposed all the way to Tara. Deep in his bones Fionn knew that, perhaps for the first time in his life, he was unafraid of meeting Goll, his men or any enemy — mortal or otherwise. He knew he was ready.

● ● ●

Finally, they reached the River Boyne and could see the Hill of Tara in the distance. It was at this location that Fionn asked his force to make camp. Once they were settled, he brought his strongest warriors together.

'We are nearly there. Tara is just over the river. Tomorrow I will enter the stronghold to meet with the High King, but I need you to stay here.'

'What? To surrender? To let you be killed?' Cnes cried. 'You expect me to stay put again, just like in Kerry? I didn't back then, and I won't this time. I came to fight for you, Fionn, but I can't fight for you from the far side of a river!'

The others joined in with their own shouts of disapproval. Fionn allowed the noise to settle before continuing.

'Cnes, you were right to come after me on Torc Mountain. I didn't know what I was up against. But this time I do — it is not a malevolent wild boar or the forces of Goll Mac Morna and those corrupted members of the Fianna who follow him. It is a fire-breathing dragon called Aillen Mac Miona, released by my grandfather, Tadg, former Chief Druid to the High King. This creature is of the Tuatha Dé Danann, and it is his revenge. It is an evil spirit that wants to end this age of mortals, and it won't stop until it destroys our High King and Tara — and everything else. No warrior has come close to killing it. If I don't defeat it, it won't matter if we change the rule of Ireland or not.'

'How will you kill it?' Crimmal asked.

'I don't know yet, but I know I have to.'

'What will happen then — after you kill it?' Cnes asked.

'Then the High King decides. He will know that I am prepared for peace but ready for war. I will ask that he give me back my rightful heritage and allow me to take over leadership of the Fianna so they will serve the people of Ireland once again. But if we all march into Tara now, there will be much bloodshed. I will go alone.'

● ● ●

Silence surrounded Conn's table. To his right sat his young son, Art. To his left, Goll. And beside Goll were his dejected warriors. The moon was waxing. Tomorrow night would bring a new moon and the arrival once more of the dragon. Since the last attack, they had rebuilt very little. Conn knew that he could not hold out on Tara much longer. People were suffering, starving and scared. They wanted someone to do something, but Conn was powerless. Everything he had tried had failed. Advice from his druids had proven worthless. Action from the Fianna proved hollow. Nothing had been able to prevent this supernatural spirit of evil from wreaking destruction.

A year and a half ago, he had been in the Great Hall celebrating Samhain with nearly a thousand men, women and children. Tonight they should be holding the feast of Bealtaine here. Instead a picture of defeat surrounded him as dejected men, sitting on whatever they could find, silently ate supper.

The Great Hall was a memory, and he knew that Tara could soon be a memory too. He realised that if he lost Tara he would lose many of the kingdoms around the country that supported him. Last year, the revolts in the Kingdoms of Kerry had shown that those who once agreed to serve under him were now unafraid to oppose him. And with rumours of forces gathering around Fionn, the son of his once-loyal servant Cumhall, he feared for the Kingdom of Ireland. If weakness set in, it would not take long for foreign rulers to invade.

Standing up and drawing all eyes towards him, he called out. 'What has become of you? What has become of us? Were we ever a proud force that could stand up to the forces that threatened us, natural or supernatural, on this island or from abroad, from our world or the Otherworld? I ask you, who will stand tall tonight and fight? On this night of Bealtaine, when we should be celebrating opportunity and hope after a long winter, who will bring the Fianna back to glory? Who will defend this ancient capital of Tara that once inspired allegiance but is now a symbol of decay? Will you, Goll, head of the Fianna? Will you battle this dragon?'

Goll looked down. He knew he could not defeat the dragon and he was not ready to die trying. Other warriors did the same, afraid to make eye contact with their king, such was their shame. But from the crowd, a voice was heard.

'I will.'

All eyes shot to a hooded figure at the back of the crowd, whom no one had noticed arrive. Conn approached the figure and placed his ceremonial horn of mead in his hand.

Conn spoke. 'Who are you? I do not recognise your voice.'

With every eye trained on him, the figure drew back his hood to reveal the youthful face of a boy.

'I am Fionn, son of Cumhall — the warrior who proudly led the Fianna before he was exiled by you, my lord, and then murdered by Goll Mac Morna. I am Fionn, son of Muirne, who has been hunted since birth from the glens of Antrim to the mountains of Kerry, from the bogs of Connemara to the coastal bays of Wicklow. I am Fionn and, despite all this, I have come to fight for you and to kill the dragon known as Aillen Mac Miona, an evil spirit of the Tuatha Dé Danann that was freed from its lair through a sidhe at Slieve Fuad by your once-loyal Chief Druid, Tadg, in order to exact his revenge. This creature is determined to destroy the capital of our island kingdom and those who live on it. I will fight this foe. All I ask is that, by the kings, chiefs, druids and poets present, you promise me that when I defeat Aillen Mac Miona, you will honour my birthright and make me the head of the Fianna.'

Upon hearing this, Goll stood up and unsheathed his sword. But Conn turned to him and commanded, 'Hide your blade. The roof of this Great Hall may no longer be above our heads, but I will not have the rules of this once great place of welcome go up in flames as well. No guest in our company will be harmed this evening!'

Goll sat down and Conn continued. 'Fionn, son of Cumhall – who was once my finest and most loyal servant – I cannot repay the debt I owe you. However, I can return your heritage to you. I promise this on my own son's life. If you defeat this malevolent monster, I will name you the head of the Fianna.' Conn then turned to Goll. 'Goll, you have led the Fianna for almost fifteen years, but this dragon now threatens the very existence of our kingdom. If you are not able to defeat this spirit, then you are bound to follow the warrior who can.'

● ● ●

After the meal, as the Fianna departed to begin the work of bringing the remaining villagers from Tara to safety, Fionn remained at the table until every seat except one was empty. The man in this seat finally stood up and approached Fionn. But, before the stranger had a chance to address him, the young warrior spoke.

'Fiacha?'

'Yes. How did you know?'

'I have a memory in which my father once spoke of you. I never met my father, so I don't know if it was a dream or a vision or if even the face that I recognise is that of my father's. But he said you would be waiting here for me.'

Fiacha felt his eyes fill with tears. 'Yes, I have been waiting for you for nearly fifteen years. I have something for you, something your father entrusted to me.' Fiacha presented Fionn with a spear with a leaf-shaped arrowhead. 'The dragon brings with it an enchanted music that sends even the strongest of us to sleep. Placing the spear to your forehead will prevent this melody from affecting you, giving you the chance to do battle with this beast. I am afraid, however, that although the spear flies as true as an apple is a fruit, I do not know how you will protect yourself against the dragon's fierce flames to get close enough to use it.'

Fionn smiled graciously and put his hand on Fiacha's shoulder. 'Don't worry, my friend. I have come this far. I trust I will find a way to go that little further.'

'I am sure you will.' Fiacha knelt before Fionn. 'I was proud to serve your father for many years. If the gods are good and we awake tomorrow and you are still alive, I would like to serve Fionn, son of Cumhall.'

'I would be honoured to lead someone whom my father put so much faith in, and I would be honoured if you became one of my trusted advisors. I demand of you just one thing – if I do become the head of the Fianna, you must promise me that you will never fear telling me I am wrong, no matter the consequences.'

'I swear.'

• • •

Fionn stood watch at the Lia Fáil, the Stone of Destiny, where every High King who had ever served in Ireland had been crowned. Here, at the very top of the Hill of Tara, as the sun set across the rolling countryside of Meath, he thought of how much his life had changed. From his sheltered childhood in the company of his foster mothers, Bodhmall and Breac, to escapes and survivals, fights and farewells. As he looked at the last rays of sun disappearing down the horizon, his heart lifted as he remembered his new friends and family – Cnes, Cana, Iollan, Crimmal and Rian. Although he was about to face his toughest foe, he no longer felt alone.

• • •

'Stay awake, Demne!'

Fionn awoke with a start and jumped to his feet. He had been keeping a keen eye to the north, where the dragon Aillen Mac Miona would come from, when everything had grown dark and his eyes had started to feel heavy. But before he was carried off to sleep his mother's voice had spoken in his ear and he had been awakened. The dragon! He could hear it more clearly now. It was the sweetest, most melodious song he had ever heard. As it neared, he could feel a dead weight pull his eyelids down again. 'Must ... get ... the ... spear,' he whispered to himself as his leaden arms reached for the weapon. He gripped it loosely and lifted it to his forehead. The song was coming closer and closer.

FLASH!

A searing clarity zoomed forth in his mind, clearing the fog that had been lulling him to sleep. And just in time, too. Flying low over the oaks, aspens, ash and elder trees, Aillen Mac Miona swooped past. Fionn was knocked from his feet, such was the force of its wings. Fionn landed heavily and had the breath knocked out of him, but he had no time to rest. Aillen Mac Miona had caught sight of him lying on the ground – with his spear out of reach. Dragons were known to have the vision of cats at night, and Aillen Mac Miona could see as clearly in the gloom as one could see in the noontime sun. In a short, sharp arc it curved down towards Fionn. As Aillen Mac Miona readied his fiery breath, Fionn regained his senses. He jumped to his feet and dived into a nearby well. Aillen Mac Miona's breath of fire began to boil the water. As the dragon again took off upwards, Fionn jumped out half-scalded. Aillen Mac Miona once again spotted him. Angered that a mortal had somehow managed to withstand his enchanted song and his flames and now dared to stand up to him, the dragon swung around to attack.

Fionn had barely caught his breath when he saw Aillen Mac Miona plunging down towards him. He could not see the spear in the murk surrounding him. Was this it? Was this how it would end? In a blaze of little glory on a hillside at Tara? On instinct, Fionn put his thumb into his mouth and suddenly remembered the magic treasure bag still hanging around his shoulder. 'Quick! Quick!' his mother's voice urged. As the tumultuous sound of Aillen Mac Miona's wings came closer, Fionn threw his hand into it and pulled out a crimson fringed cloak that he held towards Aillen Mac Miona, its nostrils now streaming fire. However, the flames did not penetrate the garment. They bounced right off it into the ground, creating a large crater.

Witnessing this mortal survive his attack again, Aillen Mac Miona grew even more enraged and swept around again and again and again to blow streams of fire at Fionn. But the cloak that Fionn held up, held firm. As dawn approached, Aillen Mac Miona grew tired and the frequency of his attacks lessened. Fionn sensed the dragon's tiredness, and in the creeping dawn light he could see where his spear had been knocked to. This was his chance. As Aillen Mac Miona circled one last time and turned for Slieve Fuad, Fionn grabbed the spear his father had left him and with all his might flung it at the dragon.

The spear flew straight and true and pierced the side of the dragon. With a monstrous shriek, it folded over in the dawn sky and crashed to earth, its life extinguished.

• • •

Conn awoke to a monstrous shriek as Aillen Mac Miona's song no longer held power over those it had put to sleep. While he found grass scorched deeply, little damage had been done to the buildings that had been standing the night before. As others awoke and returned to their homes, word spread of a great force at the western gates. When Conn arrived, he was met by Fionn Mac Cumhaill, a five-hundred-strong force and the remains of Aillen Mac Miona.

At this sight, Conn strode towards Fionn and took him in a warm embrace. 'I am sorry for all the pain and suffering I have allowed to enter your and your parents' lives. I want to ask for your forgiveness.' Conn made to kneel, but before he could, Fionn bowed.

'Do not kneel, my king. I came to serve you, and serve you I have. I ask not for your apology but for your word to make me the captain of the Fianna so that I can walk in the footsteps of my father.'

'Then rise, Fionn Mac Cumhaill, leader of the Fianna.'

All the Fianna warriors rose to proclaim their new leader. All except Goll and his men, who were now travelling northwards, determined that they would never serve under the son of their old adversary Cumhall. But Fionn did not worry about this. Not yet, anyway. Instead, surrounded by Cnes, Cana, Iollan, Crimmal, Rian and those who in time would become his new family, he smiled and laughed and hugged and was happy.

ACKNOWLEDGEMENTS

To begin, thank you to Frances, Esme, Arthur and Patrick for all their love. To my parents, Danny and Teresa, for the cups of tea and toast. To Anne-Marie and Richard for their expert advice, and to Gearóid for his translation. To Fintan, Paraic and PJ for their suggestions. To Antonia and her team of insightful book critics — Max, Dáire, Juliet, Michael, Charley, Liana and Danny (10 out of 10!). To Oísín, Emma, Caoimhe, Cian and Conor for the thumbs up.

To Deirdre, Aoibheann and the rest of the gang at Gill Books for always being so supportive.

Finally, while researching this book I read a number of fascinating texts about Fionn, and I am indebted to these authors for their wonderful work. Chief amongst those I would like to give special mention to Marie Heaney's wonderful *Over Nine Waves*.

ABOUT THE AUTHOR
AND ILLUSTRATOR

RONAN MOORE is a secondary school English teacher. When not trying to get students to stand on their desks to look at the world in a different light, he is trying to get them off their desks to take down their homework. He lives in Meath with his wife and three children.

ALEXANDRA COLOMBO is an illustrator from Bulgaria. She attended the Milan European Institute of Design and received a first-class degree in Illustration. Her great passion is writing and illustrating poems, books and fairy tales.